SHORT STORIES
for the SOUL

BOOK 1

***

PETER LUNDELL

PeterLundell.com

Peter Lundell / Lundell Publishing
20801 La Puente Road
Walnut, CA 91789
www.PeterLundell.com

Publisher's Note: This is a work of fiction. Names, characters, places, and incidents are a product of the author's imagination or are used fictitiously. Any resemblance to actual persons, living or dead, or to business establishments, institutions, events, or locales is completely coincidental.

Cover design by C.J. McDaniel, godlycovers.com

Short Stories for the Soul, Book 1 / Peter Lundell
ISBN 978-0692320396

To my mother,

who showed me the importance of

the spiritual world,

humility,

and service to others.

CONTENTS

Thank you to my critique group members Mary Kay, Lynda, and Allen. Thank you, Gayle, for your sharp eye and good questions. Thank you, Kim, my wife, who encourages me. Thank you to all gave me general feedback and who helped me get details right.

A closed mouth and an open mind go well together.

- 1 -

FAR ENCOUNTER

A mud puddle can change everything.

Sean McGregor sped his motorcycle down a narrow, rock-studded road through the Haitian countryside. Men stopped and stared, machetes hanging in their hands. Half-naked children lined up in front of mud huts and waved. Fruit-laden donkeys jittered at his engine's roar and backed up, no matter what direction they faced. Endless bumps jarred Sean's wrists and elbows, and to spare his back, he crouched bent-kneed off the motorcycle seat.

At noon he had left the Peace Corps dispensary in the North Central Plateau. Instead of taking the main road, he challenged himself with this torturous backcountry route he'd never traveled before. It was said that trucks rarely attempted it, and never cars. Perfect for two wheels—and all the more fun because he told no one he was going this way.

Port-au-Prince was at least four or five hours off. The road, along with the area's lack of cell phone coverage, gave him precious solitude—away from his coworkers and away from the Haitians.

Coming to this country was supposed to help him become a better person by serving humanity. Either the magic hadn't happened yet, or he was a slow learner. At least the overall adventure beat video games and working at 7-Eleven. And it would look good on a résumé.

His thoughts again found their way to Celeste, who had promised to wait for him in the States. She was his heaven.

Here and now he'd settle for a bit of fun, but Haiti offered little of that.

On a whim he popped a wheelie as he crested a hill. Dashing down the other side, his tires coursed into a rut.

And the rut bottomed into a mud puddle.

No!

He yanked the handlebars back, but the front tire lodged deep in the mud, as the seat surged upward, and he threw himself against the rising back end, but the rear fender kept coming, thrusting him higher, catapulting him, airborne, over a donkey, while below him the bike flipped and hit the donkey, as he kept flying, helplessly, the road rushing at him, and he crashed hard on his right shoulder.

Massive shocks reverberated through him.

This didn't happen.

His breath caught in his throat and wouldn't move.

He lay still. The motorcycle lay still. The sound of the donkey's hooves kicking in the dirt interspersed its horrified screeches.

An overhanging tree dulled to a gray blur. No air was coming in. His lungs screamed for air. Pain pierced his neck, back, and shoulder, then stabbed his whole body. Still no air. The gray blur turned black.

He lay motionless. How long, he didn't know.

Then a trickle of air seeped in, slowly increasing until his lungs were bellowing, and blackness turned to blurry gray. His head throbbed and his body quivered under the slashing pain. *Flipped. Where's bike? I'm on bike. No. Mud puddle. Donkey.*

"Blanc! Blanc! Blanc te frape bourik!" (A white hit a donkey!) Voices climbed upon each other. Sean rolled from his side onto his back, recoiling in a spasm of pain. The voices ceased, then resumed. Another voice, maybe the donkey's owner, spat like a machine gun. The donkey made no more sounds. The whole world writhed in a blur.

One voice seemed to command the others. Then several hands began to lift him, and it felt as if a knife pierced his neck. The voices calmed, and the machine gun voice burst out again. The commanding voice silenced it, and a number of hands took hold of Sean and lifted. The pain slashed with new energy. He screamed loud and long.

He stopped when they laid him on a straw mat over the uneven dirt floor of a hut. Several hands cut at the torn jacket over his bleeding shoulder and gently peeled back the fabric. His shoulder recoiled under a bath of cool water and jittered violently from a cloth wiped over it.

The benevolent torment stopped, and a hand tugged at his helmet. Sean gasped. A young woman peered down at him. He could not distinguish the details of her brown face against the dark ceiling. She and a man pulled at the helmet again. Sean screamed and touched his left hand to the helmet, motioning outward. The man and woman fumbled with the helmet and pulled. Sean screamed and repeated with his left arm. The hands fumbled, pulled outward and lifted the helmet off, over his deep gasp.

His neck down through his upper back and right arm felt as if it were on fire, knives jammed between every bone. On his junior high playground, Sean had learned not to cry. Now he wished he could because he felt fear outgrowing his pain. He hadn't met a single vehicle on the road and doubted any would venture its ruts and river crossings any time soon.

The man with the commanding voice talked above him. The woman responded agreeably to whatever it was he said. She called him "François."

The doorway filled with black heads. The air felt dead, embalmed in mixtures of smoke, dung, urine, straw, and stale beans. A small window above him permitted a beam of light to filter through.

He wondered if he was really here—*An open stretch unfolded; he shifted. A slight hill. Steeper down the other side. A donkey backed up from the edge of the road, jerking its helpless master with it. A mud puddle*—yes, he was here.

As his vision cleared, he could see that the white-washed mud walls contoured in and out and formed ridges over the supporting posts. A kitchen area and two chairs stood on one side of the room, and a door to another room stood across from the outside door. The woman wore a brown, threadbare dress, with her hair pulled back into a knot. Her teeth and the whites of her eyes contrasted her smooth brown face. She laid a cool, wet rag on his forehead and pulled his torn shirt back over the wound on his shoulder. She casually brushed away several flies. Smoke drifted in past all the staring heads and through the doorway.

The man, François, bent down to Sean. "Kote ou te sortie?" (Where did you come from?)

"La Victoire."

Voices murmured at the door.

"Corps de Paix." (Peace Corps.)

The voices talked louder.

"Kote ou te alle?" (Where were you going?)

"Port-au-Prince."

The voices quieted and the man spoke softly to the woman. The two stepped out of the hut, chasing away the onlookers as they went. Chickens cackled and clucked. Soon the woman returned, removed the rag, soaked it, and placed it back on his forehead.

Darkness slowly overtook the indistinct lines of the walls and doorway. Small tin oil lamps now flickered, and voices outside the hut seemed to keep each other company. The woman sat beside Sean and hummed softly to herself. Two boys stumbled into the room, and she abruptly shooed them out, where they whispered on the other side of the doorway to the other room.

The woman looked down on him. "Mwe rele Angelique." (My name is Angelique.) "Ii ou?"

"Sean."

"Shaann."

Sean surprised himself by smiling.

The voices outside disappeared one by one, then someone shut the door and window. François did not return. Angelique put the two boys to bed in the other room then returned and laid a straw mat beside him. She sat down, closed her eyes and began to sing. Sean couldn't make out the meaning except for "merci." Then she clasped her hands together and talked to herself, gently rocking. Perhaps she was praying.

There would have to be a god for that to be any use. And if there were one, he-she-it would have to care. Even if this god cared, the woman couldn't have much to be thankful for.

She finished and smiled. "Bon nuit." She put out the light and stepped into the other room.

Then the horrible reality pressed him like a millstone: *They're just leaving me here.*

The pain seemed to dull from ragged exhaustion. The hard, dirt floor rose slightly under the small of his back. He shifted until the ground felt flat. In the quiet, several dogs barked in the distance.

He willed himself to dredge up a good memory. *Celeste stared over a candle jammed into a Spanish wine bottle. Under the dim lights of the restaurant, the candle's glow danced across her face. Her mouth twitched at its corners, embarrassed that he should look at her when she was beginning to cry. Her eyes glistened and her voice quivered. "I'll miss you." He reached his hand, but she kept hers under the table.*

Cicadas sang steadily. They were company, but distant, unconcerned companions. Their sound ushered another memory. *Sean spoke to the pilot over the drone of the single-prop engine. Sunlight glinted off the waves of the Haitian coast, and blue turned to gray by the shore then to shades of green as the colors rose out of the sea to a wide plain with fringes climbing gently then steeply into mountains. An updraft caught the plane on its approach to a ridge. It was like sailing. A cloud floated far ahead, too far and too high. It billowed a mass of cotton up to the sun, too bright to look at. The plane would never reach it.*

One dog kept barking alone. Stupid dog—alone and barking in the dark. Sean cursed Haiti. He cursed the road and the donkey. Someone rustled in the other room, and all fell silent again. The world was black, and the pain did not sleep. All he had was his thoughts.

The wind hissed through a crack in the blackness. To someone else it was home. To him it was a tomb. Lying helplessly and wondering if he would die in a mud hut in this stinking pit of poverty had not been on Sean's job description. "Why did I ever come here?" he mumbled. "Should've never joined the Peace Corps. Should've never come here."

He wished he could sleep. He wished he could rewrite his story. *Celeste pulled a handkerchief out of her purse and wiped her eyes. "Don't cry," he said. "I'm coming home. See me fly." . . . The plane sped like a go-cart in a descent through the valley, a river twisting below. Several pillars of smoke gave away locations of mud huts on the mountainsides. The plane leveled off then began to climb—away from the huts, away from mud puddles. . . . But a donkey jerked back, its eyes glaring white. Its master yanked the rope—gaping at Sean as he flew, as he shattered.*

The pain would not sleep, and the musty stench hanging in the room grew heavier as the night dragged on. He wished someone would open the door or window. With no treatment, he might never leave this hovel. Or he might never walk again. He wished he would lose consciousness because he did not have the bravado to die.

Haiti could rot for all he cared. But then the place was already putrid. Why had he ever cared? If these people would ever learn to do anything right, they wouldn't be so poor, and the road would have been paved. No help, no communication, and no one smart enough to do anything about it.

François, with the commanding voice directing the others, was the only one who seemed to know anything. And now he had disappeared.

Then came a sound. Outside the door. Feet scraping the dirt. A muffled voice, low, not calling or talking to anyone. A single voice, chanting. Some kind of incantation. More shifting feet. Then a scratching above the door, perhaps the doorframe, something scraping or pressing into the wood. The chanting again.

Should I shout? Call Angelique?

The feet shuffled away, and the stillness returned.

There would be no point in waking her now.

He stared into the blackness and drifted. *He grabbed Celeste's hand, but it vanished in his grip. He looked at her face. She smiled and faded until he could see through her, then she disappeared. And all around the restaurant every chair sat empty. . . . The plane broke over a ridge, and a bay opened to the sea. The water sparkled in paisley patterns of currents and winds blowing contrary to currents. He turned toward the pilot, but the pilot disappeared. He looked to the back seat and no one was there. He sat alone in the plane, not knowing how to fly it. The engine's drone grew louder and louder until his mind began to shatter.*

Angelique was patting his face and holding his jaw when Sean heard himself screaming. In the black room he could see the outline of her body. A tear slipped down the side of his face. Finally. He was crying. It was easier to cry in the dark than in the daylight.

***

Sean must have fallen asleep again, because the next thing he saw was cracks of light tiptoeing on the contoured mud wall. Angelique opened the window shutter to let the morning in, along with the chorus of donkeys, dogs, guinea hens, and chickens. She hummed as she opened the door.

Then she screamed.

He defied the pain to lift his head and see. White powder lay scattered in front of the door, and the severed head of a chicken hung by a string above the frame. Angelique never stopped yelling as she trampled the powder and yanked out the nail that dangled the chicken head. Then she bolted out of sight.

He lowered his head. Behind him stood the two boys, jittery and bug-eyed with fear.

Murmuring rose all around the hut. Children appeared in the doorway and adults stood several feet behind them, some shaking their heads, others talking and gesturing. The children silently stared at Sean, their eyes wide.

Superstitious idiots.

But he had heard stories. People being cursed, getting sick, dying. He had never been the target before.

His stomach ached from a bladder nearly bursting, and he let the repulsive inevitable happen. This primeval rat hole made him urinate in his own pants—with an audience. He closed his eyes and tried not to think about it. A sniffing sound came near his warm, wet thighs. He opened one eye to a goat with an angular skull, peering down through rectangular pupils. One of the boys pulled the goat outside and returned to stare at Sean. The adults began pointing at him as they chattered.

He hated every single one of them. He hated the whole country.

Angelique returned, quiet and angry. She swept the powder away with harsh strokes of the spindly broom then slammed the door on the observers. As if Sean and the two boys weren't there, she began shouting into the ceiling. The boys fell to their knees. She placed her hands on each of their heads then on Sean, shouting the whole time.

She finished, turned to him, and spoke rapid fire, apparently explaining. He caught some of the words: donkey dead, owner angry, voodoo, Sean . . . dead.

"Superstition," he told himself. "That's all it is."

He could hear her breathing.

"That's all it is. Nothing more. Right?"

She paced the room.

He pretended to not feel the anxiety shivering through him.

She stopped and stood over him, her eyes glowering. She sure seemed to take that stuff seriously, but she didn't look afraid. Only mad. She was different from the others.

She paced again and talked more calmly at the ceiling until she eventually stood still and silent, then said, "Amen."

She brought a dish of rice and beans, and with a tarnished spoon proffered it to Sean. His nose crinkled, but his stomach was empty. She lifted his head to receive a spoonful, he gasped in pain, then chewed slowly so as not to choke. She tipped a tin cup of water over his lips, letting half the water run down his neck; the rest he gagged on and swallowed. She frowned in understanding, rose, and went outside.

He thought of his father who had contracted amoebic dysentery after drinking the water on a trip to Africa.

In the full daylight he could see that the roof was made of straw, and spindly lengths of twisted wood spanned the room along the tops of the walls. On them lay a few sawed planks on which rested woven baskets. A cockroach skittered down a wall. He lifted his left arm to smash it but could not reach.

Without her, the room itself felt abandoned. The sun rose higher in the sky, stoking the day's heat in this thatch-roofed oven.

He wondered where his motorcycle was.

The weakest of breezes struggled through the little window. Someone was chopping wood. Each strike of the ax jabbed at him. He began to cry again. He wanted Angelique to come back. He might have called her poor, but somehow it didn't seem like the right word anymore.

One of the boys pushed open the door. He was eating a mango, and the juice oozed down his face and hands. Angelique came in and sat down with a cup of water and a small plastic bowl of cornmeal. The cornmeal was bland, but he was too hungry to care anymore. She tipped the cup to the corner of his mouth rather than the center so less water would be lost, and the little that escaped felt cool across his cheek. He choked only three times before he finished. Angelique smiled and held the smaller boy.

A man appeared in the doorway and spoke harshly—the machine gun voice. Angelique stood and shouted at him. He spat back a sharp rebuke. They screamed at each other. At the same time. And did not stop. Then the man quieted and nodded.

She must have told him off. Sean smiled.

After the man left, she babbled at Sean again: Donkey's owner. Wanted money. No, Angelique said, no money. Take motorcycle.

"Take the— My motorcycle? How could you—" Sean groaned loudly.

"Shhh." She sat and covered his forehead with her hand.

The smaller boy sat on her lap.

A cheerful voice came from outside, and two people approached, carrying buckets of water. Angelique thanked them and stepped outside to talk.

Sean clenched his teeth. *How could that stupid woman give away my bike? Why can't these people . . .*

No.

Honesty check.

A donkey was a man's livelihood. Sean would probably never ride the motorcycle again anyway.

He was the one who had popped a wheelie without seeing what was on the other side of the hill.

Angelique had given him hours of attention.

These people had brought water.

Angelique dabbed a wet rag on his face and body again. It occurred to Sean that the whole time he had lain there, she had done very few of the daily chores Haitian women always do. He smiled at her, and she smiled back.

Shackled by the constant pain, Sean faded into a delirium as the sun faded into evening. *The clouds billowed high and white. He tried to reach them but could not. He only felt himself falling through empty space, reaching, groping—grasping only air. Falling, helpless, he hit the ground hard, much too hard.*

A stabbing shiver ran through him.

Tip-taps spread across the thatched roof. The sky rumbled over the descending darkness, and the rain fell harder, soon hushing all other sounds. An oil lamp flickered for a while, casting shadows around the room that was once again shut up like a tomb. Drops randomly fell through the roof, some on his body. Angelique was talking again, or praying, rocking gently. The oil lamp went out, and there was only the rain. Sean wished the rain would wash him away.

Though he was weak from hunger, eating was too painful. If it weren't, Angelique would certainly have fed him continually. He felt his body slipping, as if into a hole.

What felt like a temporary death cradled Sean through much of the night. If he awoke in the morning, he would receive life back again. He only didn't want to be permanently maimed like too many he'd seen. The memory now became a nightmare: *At the village market a man with a humpback approached him with hand outstretched, palm up. His arm was contorted from broken bones having never been set. Another man walked with the help of a crutch. His left leg was shorter than the right, and the foot turned up and in so that he actually walked on his ankle. Sean tried to turn away, but he was bent and twisted just like them.*

His eyes flashed open, he was breathing hard. He was afraid to sleep but too exhausted to stay awake. Sometime in the night the rain stopped, and the creeping quietness made the darkness empty again. No one knew where he was. Lost in this hut on the far edge of nowhere—and no one would find him. But death knew where he was. It crept toward him.

The cicadas revived and serenaded the black emptiness, as if to keep death at bay. Sean surprised himself by wishing Angelique were awake to pray or whatever it was she did. Death had no right to take him yet. But in the clinics he had seen death care nothing for rights. Permanent disfigurement cared nothing either. A person had no rights. A person had only hope, and sometimes not even that.

The darkness felt like a death shroud, wrapping him in a quiet, sinister menace. His neck, back, and shoulder continued to register knives twisting in his wounds. He blinked hard to hold back the delirium of exhausting pain.

Celeste, his heaven. He would think of Celeste. *Walking on a beach, sun shining, his hand in hers, wind wafting their hair. She smiled. He smiled and smiled and smiled. They splashed in the waves. She skipped ahead and turned, arms wide to embrace him. He raised his hand to her. But she backed up and kept backing out of reach. His legs would not move. She kept backing. Waves washed higher on his legs then his waist. Her arms lowered and her smile faded. Another wave bashed him off his feet. She kept fading. He floundered in the surf, gasp-*

ing for air. She disappeared. A final wave battered him in a stinging salt burial and sucked him out to oblivion.

He awoke with a gasp. His eyes opened to the blackness, which was no different from his keeping his eyes shut.

Escape was an illusion. Alone in a tomb, but for Angelique. She would at least distract him and maybe keep death away until daylight. He began to call her, but only wearied breath passed his lips. He tried again, "Angelique." But he heard no stirring in the other room.

If he were at a threshold, it would not be for her to hold him back. No one could do that. A man, even a young fool, had to face his fate.

Afraid to die and afraid to live, Sean began to cry. He wept gently and quietly; anything more was too painful on his neck. And finally, "Dear God." He hoped there was one. And he kept weeping. "Dear God" was all he knew to say.

Sometime in the night he saw himself lying beside a well. In his mind's eye he gripped a rope with a bucket on the end that carried what was his life. As if by his decision, he could hold on or let go.

The rope chafed his hand. The memories, desires, and assumptions that filled the bucket were heavier than he had imagined. The vision grew clearer. Everything in the bucket was about him, what he had, what he wanted, and even coming to this poor country to prove what a good person he was.

But he might never walk again, never hold Celeste. Or maybe he would. And he wondered if it really mattered either way.

The rope slipped. His breath grew shallow. He could live or die with little difference between the two.

He let go.

The end.

For a moment he stopped breathing and no longer had the strength to care.

But his breath fought back and kept him alive.

Perhaps he would last the night. He would await his fate in the daylight.

The cicadas quieted, and all was still.

One last time he whispered, "Dear God." Sean slipped into sleep. He did not dream, and he did not strain toward what was out of reach.

All was silent and black.

***

The morning sun shone through the open window, and the neighborhood donkeys, dogs and chickens howled their usual cacophony. Angelique was singing softly in the other room. One of the boys got up from a chair and went in to her. She came out smiling, still wearing the same threadbare dress she had at the beginning, probably her only one.

The miserable hut convinced Sean he was still alive. Whether that was good or not, he couldn't decide.

But something was different.

She scooped something out of a pot and into the plastic bowl then sat down to spoon-feed him. Rice gruel. Grimacing in pain, he choked and ate several mouthfuls without worrying about bacteria.

She was the same, but he wasn't.

Her chocolate brown hand was hard-work rough yet tender-woman slender. This hand had certainly never worn a diamond, never driven a car, never lifted a crystal glass. Instead it held the spoon that fed him—with love and no complaint.

She had not asked for Sean to crash his bike and end up on her dirt floor. He had invaded her life. Yet she gave whatever she could.

He watched her hands scoop another small spoonful of gruel.

Had he been listening all his life to the wrong definitions of wealth and poverty?

Now he could see. After all this time he could finally see.

She was not poor.

He was.

The realization pressed upon him like a hand squeezing out of his heart and mind every false pretense he had carried. His lips trembled. His eyes began to water, until tears streamed down both sides of his face, even though it was daylight.

She peered down at him, puzzled.

If Sean had died the previous night, he would've died a poor man. But he had not died. So it was not too late. He would not miss this chance. He blinked back the tears and looked at Angelique.

She leaned toward him, concern in her eyes.

He marveled at the richness in her poverty. Yet it was more. It was *her*—who she was in the midst of it. She loved. And she gave her love without measure. She was maybe the richest person he had ever known.

He wanted that. More than he wanted to get well, more than he wanted Celeste, he wanted what Angelique had. He had no idea what to do, but he knew where to start. He cleared his throat. "Padon mwe." (Forgive me.)

She wrinkled her eyebrows, obviously not understanding. He didn't try to explain.

He closed his eyes and let the tears flow again. "Padon mwe."

She spoke softly, something about his not having to feel sorry. She rose and took the plastic bowl then returned with a cup of water. He drank most of it.

Sean gazed intently at her until his eyes held hers. "Merci."

She smiled and cocked her head to one side. "Pa de qua." (You're welcome.)

The knives kept stabbing and twisting as the morning aged into another day of torment. The sun's rays slanted higher, and the heat found its way back in. He didn't mind so much any more.

While Angelique dabbed the wet rag on him again, her head popped up.

Then Sean heard it. A rumbling sound, turning to drumming—thumping, steadily pounding. It gradually grew louder, along with a high-pitched mechanical whine. It was moving, coming closer.

"Li vini!" (They're coming!) "François vini!" She beamed at him and ran out the door.

The drumming grew louder. Louder. The hut began to vibrate, and Sean felt the staccato beat of air pressure. A helicopter hovered overhead.

Beauty fades, but not its source.

- 2 -

THE DANCER

Are my body parts being robbed, or am I just living too long? Grace let the door shut behind her. She laid the mail on the kitchen table and sat down, then pulled off her shoes and massaged her feet in circular motions, one at a time, the way her doctor had shown her. The walk through the apartment halls to the mailbox and back had grown more painful since last spring. Her heart sank just a little every time she looked at the stairs, which she hadn't climbed since summer. She was reduced to thinking, *Thank God for elevators. Or thank the guy who invented them.*

As she rubbed, she stared at the numbers of the calendar hanging on the refrigerator door. They seemed alternately friends and enemies, depending on what she was enduring or anticipating. Thanksgiving was circled in red. The kids would have her over, but this year was different. Ralph couldn't go. And she didn't want to go without him. Everyone would argue about it and then feel bad because they all loved each other too much to exclude anyone or to skimp on a holiday together. But they couldn't very well do a full turkey dinner in a nursing home. *And what would be the point,* someone would finally say. Ralph could barely feed himself.

She'd think about it later.

Three pieces of mail this time: A phone bill. *Okay.* A letter from a credit card company: "0% for six months!" *My lucky day*—trash. And an oversize post card advertisement for *The Nutcracker* on December 7–22. *Hmmm . . .* Next to "A holiday tradition your family will treasure!" the Nutcracker himself wore a big paper-mache head with his right leg tucked and left leg extended in a *pas de chat* leap. Grace turned the card over, sure of what she'd see on the back. Yes, the requisite Mouse King threatened from the side, and the Sugar Plum Fairy smiled in a *pas de deux* with the Prince.

"Should I really go back again?" she whispered to herself and looked blankly at the linoleum floor tiles. The refrigerator hummed, and the air from the bottom vent warmed her feet.

She nodded, hobbled to the couch, sat, and pulled an old album from under the end table. There, a third of the way through and frozen in time, shined the old promotion photo. Her own position, all the way up to her fingertips, was the same as that of the young woman in the advertisement. Grace smiled and traced her finger across her photograph then over several other shots of her performances.

She closed her eyes with a long breath and saw the stage, the other dancers, the audience, the orchestra. . . . She imagined herself surrounded by the blur of whirling bodies in the rush of crescendos. She could feel her toes pressing into the box tips of her slippers as she spun a *pirouette*. Then she leaped, legs spread, in a *grand jeté* beside the prince.

She opened her eyes and felt almost breathless.

After years that lost count, and despite her body's being ready for the recycle bin, the dance was still inside her. It wasn't merely her imagination. She could *feel* it.

She closed her eyes again, and the sensation held her, as if suspended above the couch. Maybe she shouldn't have been so surprised because she had always *felt* the dance more than seen it. It came from inside.

She sensed her feet sweep in a *glissade*, lifting swift and light. The stage was air to her.

As if lifting a shroud from her own body, she found the memories still engraved into every muscle, though the years had obscured them. She felt herself float in midair, moving fluid and free. Even the music came back the way it had once flowed through her like her own blood. Her movements and the melodies each became an expression of the other.

So. She smiled. *We really are fearfully and wonderfully made.*

After gliding and twirling a while longer, she sighed and opened her eyes. The next leaf of the album displayed her as Odette in *Swan Lake*. After that *The Sleeping Beauty*, *Cinderella*, and *Peter Pan*. She pulled out a second album. The productions and years continued until they came to her own studio and little ballerinas in training. Page after page of smiling protégés posed with her standing behind them like a proud and prodigious mother. She sighed.

The progressing dates saw her hair graying and her body growing thicker. But they did not reveal the stiffness that set in, though the declining numbers of students offered a clue. When the arthritis got too painful to demonstrate positions and moves, she did the hardest thing she'd ever done in her life and sold the studio. She wasn't a businesswoman who could hire others. She was an artist who shared herself, and she'd lost her ability to share.

It took a year before she completely stopped crying.

The worst feeling was that she no longer had the dance in her—as if age and arthritis had grown on her like a cast, like a tomb. The sense of loss wasn't just that of vocation, it was an emptiness of self.

But now she wondered if the dance had been in her all along, and she'd never thought to adapt it to an aging body.

The album still on her lap, she leaned back and dozed. Somewhere between waking and sleeping, her memory cleared itself the way she'd once cleared clutter in the attic. *Was that first performance in first grade or second?* She wore a pink tutu, Mrs. Johnson coaching her from the wings, Mom and Dad in the audience, beaming at her. She tripped over her own feet and fell but got right back up as if nothing happened and kept going—the way Mrs. Johnson taught her. And when everyone clapped at the end, they too seemed to pretend she hadn't fallen, or at least they forgave her. Then and there something in her knew that's what she wanted to do the rest of her life.

And so she did.

Almost.

Now she only danced in her dreams. She drifted back to the stage—

Brringg! Brringg! The phone rang her awake.

A quarter till two, claimed the wall clock.

That'll be Carol.

She slid the album off her lap and groaned her way up. Her knees felt stiff every time she rose. Balancing herself with a chair, she gently bent one knee then the other.

Sixth ring—"Hi, whoever you are. Leave a message for Grace, and make sure you have a good day." *Beep.*

"Hi, Mom! Are you there? Can you pick up? Hello-o-o? I'll be there in ten minutes. Mom?"

Grace lifted the handset. "I'm here. I'll be in front. . . . Yes . . . Okay . . . See you." She replaced the handset and turned toward the closet for her coat. *Beep.* Arms in, coat on. *Beep.* One beep was fine; incessant beeps drove her mad. She deleted the message and looked out the window at the black skeletons of trees clawing the overcast sky. In the summer they had been so beautiful. Just like her.

Carol waved as she pulled up to the building entryway. Grace buckled herself in as her daughter leaned over to hug her. Though the heater had warmed the car, Grace kept her gloves on. The air inside was still cool enough to give her a cruel handshake that didn't let go.

Off they went toward Highway 61.

The airflow of the heater and the tires on the road weren't musical, but Grace closed her eyes and let herself absorb their sound and feel. Finally she opened her eyes and said, "Carol, when we see your father today, I want you to imagine how he was when I first met him."

"Wasn't that at a disco?"

"My friends dragged me there. I still marvel at how a place so vulgar could yield a treasure like him."

"Swept you off your feet, didn't he?"

"No one in those places knows how to dance. They jump up and down like monkeys, wag their bodies like hyperactive dogs, and call it dancing. If I'd done my stuff there, I'd have nailed them in the gut and knocked them all over."

"You probably would have hit them lower down and had them singing like choirboys." Carol burst into giggles.

"Stay on the road, dear."

Carol calmed herself to a snicker. "Yes, ma'am."

"Your dad wasn't just more handsome than the others. He was more refined."

"Like in your wedding photos."

"Yes. But there was more." She could almost feel it even as she said it. "The way he held me. The way I felt in his arms, as if his heart and mine engaged in deep conversations whether he and I spoke anything or not."

"Mom, you've never said that before." She turned off the highway to County Road E.

Grace observed the passing burger joints and discount stores. Some things were too sacred to reduce to the banality of speech. But now Ralph could barely talk. And who knew when some calamity would take her down too.

She turned to Carol and held a steady smile. Many more things her daughter would need to hear.

Carol glanced back. "What?"

"How many things between you and your own husband happen without words?"

"Hmmm . . . Probably a lot more than I realize." She stopped for a red light. "Before you tell me, I'll just say it: That's something I need to think about."

Grace smiled and gazed absently at the other cars. The light turned green.

"This non-verbal communication thing. Is that one reason you and Dad went ballroom dancing so often?"

"I suppose. I didn't like fishing much—slimy creatures. Leeches and worms for live bait." She shuddered.

"So he fished by himself or with the guys."

"When you were young, yes. After you were on your own, I sometimes went along just to be with him."

"But you didn't put leeches on hooks."

"I did not."

Carol changed lanes and turned left. "Dad's the only man I know who both fished and ballroom danced."

"It was the middle ground between a man who couldn't do ballet, and a woman who couldn't stand disco."

"How many ballroom competitions did you win?"

"Oh, ten or twelve. Just local and regional ones. We mainly danced for fun."

Carol shook her head. "And I could barely get past the beginner steps in your studio."

Grace smiled. "You were . . ."

"Clumsy."

Grace smiled and patted Carol's leg. "But you're a fine teacher. How many kids will grow up and thank you for changing their lives?"

"I have no idea."

"Lots, I'm sure."

Carol gently gripped her mother's gloved fingers. They rode quietly the rest of the way.

ST. CLAIRE CARE CENTER WELCOMES YOU read the sign that stood like a sentry in front of this place that Grace couldn't stand, yet still thought of living in just to be with Ralph. She climbed out of the car and hobbled in while Carol parked.

Past the smiling nun at the reception desk and the statue of St. Claire herself, Grace made her way across the lobby and into the hallway. She smiled at each wheelchaired resident. Some smiled back, others stared into space, a few hunched like shells of former humans. Carol caught up with her, and they reached Room 134, just past the busy nurse's station.

Ralph sat fully dressed in his chair between his bed and the door. Grace had made sure the staff knew better than to leave him in a bathrobe. His wifeless roommate sprawled on the opposite bed, the man's privacy curtain partly drawn. Between the beds a window opened to a courtyard of gray concrete under gray-barked, leafless trees. Ralph's curtain was pulled back, as always, and above the bed's head loomed the requisite crucifix. It attached to the wall by a pair of screws going through each of Jesus' hands. Grace could never figure out if that was the manufacturer's oversight or an act of pragmatism, a theological metaphor or devilish sarcasm.

She grasped Ralph's left hand and held it. His head quivered as he raised it toward her. He lifted the left side of his mouth into a half smile. The right half, along with the entire right side of his body, lay limp in a permanent droop.

With slurred speech he garbled, "I-I'm so glad t' see yeh."

"I'm glad to see you too, honey."

Above Ralph's medication-covered dresser, surrounded by beige walls, a dozen ballroom trophies squeezed together on a shelf. Grace had insisted he have them all. Seeing them now, she longed to go back and do it all again. When Ralph had his stroke, the whole family did everything they could, but it was as if Ralph had half died. In fact he did. And part of Grace died with him.

Carol pulled up a chair for her mother before sitting on the bed.

"Thank you, dear."

Normally the two would chat about the weather and what Carol's kids were up to, while Ralph nodded. And they would hold hands half the time just because that's what they did.

Today Grace kept looking up at the poster-size framed photo on the wall above the length of Ralph's bed. She rose and stood in front of it.

"Mom, what's with you today? That picture hung on your wall for decades."

"Good thing it's hanging here now."

Carol tilted her head forward, eyes fixed inquisitively.

"That was in Chicago. You can tell we were doing the Foxtrot. The lunge with the dip."

"And . . . ?"

"The waltz was closest to ballet, but I confess . . . the Tango was fun."

"Mom." Carol raised her eyebrows. "What gives?"

"Hard to believe I wore such sexy dresses."

"Pffft! You were the hottest mom on the block."

"Yup," Ralph rasped. "Sh-she was."

They both turned to him, mouths open in silent laughter.

The left side of his mouth twitched upward. And Grace remembered. This attempt at a grin was a ghost of the way he used to mischievously snicker when he did something Grace asked him not to do, like belching or replacing kitchen utensils in the wrong place. And she was back in the kitchen of their big house by the lake, scolding him and waiting to hear him say he loved her anyway then embrace her in his big arms.

"Mo-o-om! What's going on?"

Grace realized her face was locked in a vacant stare. She blinked herself back, then stepped close to Carol, coaxed her to her feet, and laid a hand on Carol's chest. "If something's inside you, you don't have to lose it. Even if you can't do something anymore, it's still inside you."

They held each other's gaze.

Then Grace turned. "Ralph. Let's dance."

He looked at her. His lips started moving. Eventually the words came out. "What 're y'- talkin' b-'bout?"

"You and me, buster. We're going dancing."

Ralph strained his head to the left, seeming to look for someone else she was speaking to.

She took the handles of the wheelchair and rolled him into the hallway toward the lobby.

"Mom," Carol called from behind.

Grace kept walking.

Carol came up beside her and whispered, "Mom, what are you doing?"

"Just what I said."

"But you— I mean—"

Grace turned the chair into the doorway next to the sign "Activity Room" and turned on the lights. "Sorry I didn't come prepared, Ralph. We'll just have to be spontaneous. Carol, you can be the audience."

"Okay." With a curious look Carol sat on a chair.

"Just don't do disco."

As Carol bit down on a smile, Grace glanced at the open doorway to make sure no one else was watching then pulled the wheelchair back to face Ralph's left side.

"And by the way, I'm bringing him for Thanksgiving."

She let Carol keep her wide-eyed reaction, leaned close to her husband, and looked into his eyes. "Ralph. The dance. The dance is still inside me. It's still there. I felt it today."

He looked at her as if not comprehending.

"I'll bet it's inside you too. It must be." With both hands she held his face. "We need to find it."

He furrowed the left side of his brow.

Mimicking dance moves of a lifetime ago, she said, "We're in a ballroom. They're playing a waltz. Can you feel me in your arms?"

He squinted his left eye.

"Okay. Go back with me. I'm in that red satin dress you liked so much. The strapless one with the slit in front. Remember?" She waited. "Can you see it?"

He paused, his mouth hanging open. Then he nodded. "Beau-beau'ful."

"Yes. My hand is on your shoulder. Yours is against my shoulder blade. Our feet are ready to prance with the music. Can you feel it, Ralph?"

A glimmer of recognition crossed his eyes. He lifted the left half of his mouth.

Grace smiled back and stepped behind him to take the wheelchair handles. Ralph laboriously lifted his left hand to hold hers.

She pushed the wheelchair forward then pulled back. "One, two, three . . ." Angled forward and back again. "Two, two, three. Three, two, three . . ." Until she completed a square. Then an angle forward and over. Then around as she turned the chair. The left side of his mouth was still smiling.

She began humming "Tennessee Waltz" and continued pushing the wheelchair forward, back, and around. She ignored the pain in her feet and kept moving. Ralph's hand on hers squeezed as tightly as she knew he could.

"Underarm turn now. I guess I'll have to play the guy." She held his left hand and circled it over his head as she shuffled around the chair, back to the handles.

Then she sensed it. At first she doubted, but the feeling kept coming. His heart whispered to hers, like a long-lost lover who had finally found her again. Hers whispered back. And together they slipped through a warp of time and space—gliding and spinning, across a ballroom floor, chandeliers above them, music coursing through their veins, feet in harmonious stride.

And there was no such thing as time.

They danced and danced.

Now humming "Edelweiss," she reduced her pace and kept shifting forward and back, turning in quarters, then labored through a slow motion *pirouette*.

Her feet screaming and throbbing in pain, she grudgingly stopped. Carol was holding a soaked tissue under reddened eyes.

Grace forced a smile and stepped in front of Ralph. A tear trickled down his cheek, and he smiled back with the side of his mouth that still worked. He never let go of her hand.

"You felt it, didn't you, Ralph?"

He nodded. And she caressed his face.

She drew close to him, touched noses, and pressed her lips to his.

We can never escape our greatest enemy
or our greatest friend.
Both call from within.

- 3 -

IN THE RING

I clenched my tired fists. Sweat soaked the leather inside the bulbous gloves, and I couldn't remember when I'd last taken them off.

High-intensity lights glared down from a broad ceiling. A square of three taut ropes surrounded me, a mat at my feet. Beyond that everything was gray. In front of me stood my opponent.

I swung and struck him. A weak hit, but I forgave myself for that. Hits lose strength as they lose count.

He did not strike back. He was a tricky one. He would never hit directly, never let me see it coming. The punch always came from the side, seemingly out of nowhere. Let my fist down and *bam!* I'd take a smack across my face.

I hated him for it.

But I was tired. Tired of trying to look happy while I was hitting and being hit. Tired of not knowing why I was fighting or how it would end. Tired of not going anywhere.

I wore three chains around my neck, and they weighed heavy on my shoulders. Anger, frustration, and unforgiveness will do that. I thought to take them off but they defined who I was.

No bell sounded to end the round, and I couldn't remember when it had started. After it, others would start and drag on until I collapsed and died.

That wasn't such a bad thought. At least I'd be done.

But anxiety over what would happen to my soul kept me on my feet. Whether based on fact or fiction, I feared whatever might be done to me after I died. I'd probably get stuck even more under my adversary's control than I was in this ring.

So I kept fighting.

**

Strange how days turn into weeks, months, years, and wondering what we did all the while. I had not left the ring for years and had forgotten what it was like not to fight. I often collapsed and slept. When I awoke, he was always there.

My hands were raw from endless rubbing inside the gloves. Traces of blood on my wrists told why my hands stung and felt so slimy. And accumulated grime was certainly causing infection.

I had paced the ring until I wore a visible path. And when I didn't swing at my opponent, I flailed against the ropes. Stupid, wasted effort. But I did it anyway, even as I berated myself.

My steps were slowing and my swings were weakening. I couldn't go on forever. I stared at my adversary, whom I loved and hated—which left me feeling always alone.

He faced me, eyes wide and fixed on mine.

"I'm sick of what's going on," I said.

His gaze seemed kind, even compassionate, but I didn't believe it.

I raised my fist at him. "You allowed every disaster in my life to happen. You could stop them, but you keep letting them happen."

Surrounded in a gray world of numbing repetition, the two of us faced off day after day. But now I would have it out with him. I would drain my last bit of strength. One last time to either set things straight or walk away from the whole brawl. I wanted a result. And if I died in the process, so be it. I deserved more than I got. I was done with being nice, being good, being patient. That just covered up the intolerable. No more putting up with it.

"You don't care," I said. "If you did, you'd have resolved this fight and made everything better by now."

Silence.

"But you didn't." I thought to seethe, but I sighed and waited. "You—You don't even respond."

No reply, not the slightest body movement. I may as well have faced a statue.

I began pacing left, then right, then left again, all the while my eyes on that impassive face. I pointed my glove. "You're not worth believing in!"

Nothing.

"People talk about you. They sing about you. Give their money to you. Obey what you teach in your book." I stopped and leaned toward him. "And *still* bad things happen to them."

My adversary let me say whatever I wished without retorting, without striking me down. I wished he would level me with one blow. Or at least scream at me, assail me with lightning bolts, smash me to the mat. Anything but this. I had struggled with him far too many years. I had yelled and kicked, questioned and cursed—yet he stood as if I had not.

"People turn their backs on you, and you *still* do nothing."

My broken family. Failed dreams. Countless wrongs against me. Tragedies. He had allowed it all. Some would say he caused it because he was in charge of everything. I didn't know what to believe. But I refused to believe in anyone who was behind so much disaster, so much evil.

The trouble was I wanted to believe. I needed to believe.

I argued with myself every day that I was a fool to not walk away. But something always pulled me back. I tried to ignore it, but deeper down I knew I needed it. I needed him, my adversary, even though he drove me to madness.

Without him I would be alone in my world, my boxing ring. Gloves on my hands with no one to hit and chains around my neck with no one to blame.

Yet as he stood so still, I felt alone anyway. I might as well have been. That's what made me mad. And he deserved to be hit.

"I'll show you I can run my own life better than you can, with all your empty promises and iron-fisted expectations." I cocked my arm. One good punch with everything I had left.

He stood as still as before.

"You won't defend yourself because you *can't*."

He raised his arm. Finally some movement.

Now I'll strike.

His arm arced away from the ring and slowly swept right to left. The gray that surrounded the ring swirled like a wind-blown cloud. It thinned and quickly dissolved.

All around me appeared other rings just like mine. In each one was another person: a man, a woman, a child, a senior citizen. Beyond them emerged more rings with more people of every race and age and appearance. They wore suits and dresses, jeans and shorts; glittered jewelry hung from some, rags from others. Some were in uniforms, others in wheelchairs.

They each had their own adversary.

My arms dropped to my sides. In every direction the rings spread as far as I could see. Each one different, each one hosting a fight.

"What?"

He said nothing.

"Who are they?"

"People like you."

"They're not like me."

"Think what you like."

"I will." I squinted, trying to discern the other adversaries. "And that's you? Multiplied across every ring?"

"Some of them, yes. Others, no."

I turned slowly and watched people hit their adversaries. Some were stoic like mine and did not hit back. Others were monsters that snarled and bit then crushed the people into the mat. Several looked just like the people themselves and hit first.

"Who are the other adversaries?"

"You know."

I did.

People wrestled with addictions, demons, and their own twisted selves. *Pathetic* came to mind. I banished the thought; they were too similar to me.

I squinted and looked closer. The rings with the monsters still had adversaries like mine standing on the outside, leaning on the ropes, looking in. Whether in or out of the rings, my adversary was everywhere.

I closed my eyes. Those people would have their own conflicts no matter what I did. I had to finish my own fight. And I would leave my adversary no excuses or exceptions.

"Where did they come from?"

"They were there all along." He frowned. "Fighters like yourself are unaware of others—until they're shown."

So besides everything else, he apparently wanted me to feel guilty about that. I shoved the thought aside, looked back at him, clenched my fist, adjusted my chains, and stepped forward. Even if he wouldn't fight back, I would show him my fury.

A glove swung at me, hit me across the face and sent me staggering.

What? Where did that . . .

I regained my balance and a happy rage surged through me. The trickster had gotten me again, but I had my fight. Win or lose I would swing and punch until I had nothing left.

I re-cocked my arm to strike back.

But my adversary was leaning against the ropes across the ring. I hesitated. Thought. And grew confused. He had been there all along, too far away to strike me.

He didn't have rubber-band arms. No lightning bolt had struck. It was a glove.

Perhaps another opponent had hit me. Someone from one of those other rings. I spun around to check but found no one else.

Another blow to my face. Hard, from the same direction. This time I saw it. But it made no sense. I staggered, dazed, my head throbbing.

This couldn't have happened. The punch had come from beside me. Up close. Too close.

No. Impossible.

My adversary's eyes met mine. He nodded.

"No," I said.

"Yes."

"I don't believe it."

"It is true. I'm sorry for what you put yourself through." He paused. "But now you see."

I stared at each of my arms. The striking glove was my own.

***

I blanked out for an instant, or maybe a long time, not sure if I had lost consciousness or gained a new one. I was still the same but was not the same. I now understood what I had not known before.

And the object of my anger—the one whom I'd hit, protested, and questioned—stepped toward me. His arms were slightly open, and he wore no gloves.

I instinctively drew back and raised a glove.

We stood motionless. I sensed he knew every fear and anger that knotted my heart—and every reason. It was as if he looked inside me. I wondered if he knew me better than I did. He couldn't possibly like me. I didn't even like myself.

Yet he did not chastise me, and seemed to wait only for me to lower my glove.

I did.

He extended his hand.

I turned my back and gripped the rope. I couldn't stop the fight so easily. I had too much to fight about. But I couldn't go on. The chains around my neck had grown thicker and were now so heavy I lurched. Yet I couldn't take them off, wouldn't take them off.

I glanced back. Still he held out his hand. "My wings for your gloves and chains."

"Wings?"

"The freedom to rise out of this ring. A higher place to walk, sometimes to soar, with me."

"You want me to give up my chains?"

"Yes."

"I'm right to be angry, frustrated, and unforgiving."

"Without all that you will be able to become someone new."

"Even if I do, I'll keep my gloves. I still need to fight."

"No, you don't. You need to lose."

"Yeah. So you can punish me."

"No. So you can win."

I hated how he didn't make sense. Happened all the time. "I'll win by winning. That's why I keep fighting. . . . Or is it?" I felt dizzy.

"You must let me win; only then can you win. And you will. I could force you, but I want you to choose."

"If I do go along with you, I won't believe everything will be happy."

"It won't be. But you will be different. The fight will be different because you will be free and able to fly."

Former fighters had told me about flying, but they weren't like me, and they didn't know me.

His eyes penetrated mine. "You cannot fly with chains weighing you down."

"You know, don't you?"

"Everything about you. And about what you could be."

"Why do you care?"

"Because you are mine."

"Is it because I'm yours that you let my life go through . . ." *Stop it. It doesn't do any good to replay the details. And besides, you hit yourself, remember?*

He had carefully let me have my space, my precious self-important space, just as he had always done.

One thing I had to know. "The hits I took all this time—they weren't all from me, were they?"

"A few were from me, to keep you out of trouble. Many were from your true adversary."

I squinted at him.

"Don't you remember? The monster who snarled and bit and crushed you into the mat. You saw him in some of the other rings."

"That wasn't you?"

He shook his head. "I hit you to get you back on your feet. He hits to knock you down." Then he smiled. "And besides, I'm not that ugly."

"Why didn't you ever say anything? You let me misunderstand you for so long."

"The truth has already been revealed. It is yours to discover."

"Even if people fight you or turn their backs?"

"Most of the hits you took were from your own hand. Those hurt me as much as when you hit me or turned your back on me."

"How much did I hit myself?"

"More and longer than you imagine."

I stared at the mat, trying to comprehend.

"Have you had enough?"

Yes, enough. Beyond enough. Wings were better than chains. I bent forward to let the weights slide over my head. They stuck. His hand whisked them off and dropped them to the mat in one tangled heap.

The gloves too, even if I have doubts. The hope he offers is enough. I bit at the laces on one glove to undo the knot. I threw it down, untied and threw off the other. My raw, infected hands glistened with blood.

He stretched his now-gloveless hands. They were pierced. And glistened with blood.

He embraced me.

And I embraced him, the Lover of my soul.

At the end of the logical argument I did not find Truth.

I found only a period.

He—Truth—calls me beyond myself.

- 4 -

TURNING POINT

Sophie cringed at the smell of medicine and reached into her Louis Vuitton purse for her Eau de Cartier. She sprayed a bit on her neck and wrists then hesitated in the doorway. A curtain shielded the bed. The lights were off, and the TV loomed silently.

She gripped her purse handles tightly with her right hand, mindful of the bandage around the scrapes on her swollen left hand. Her nail polish remained remarkably intact.

Deep breath.

What would she say? If he were asleep, she could just sit silently.

She closed her eyes and composed herself, then entered.

Rounding the curtain, she gasped at the sight of him and instinctively raised her free hand to her mouth. Just as quickly she lowered it to the mattress to steady herself. She bent forward, mouth open, breath halted. She fixed her eyes on the thin, sky blue blanket that lay flat under her hand, where his legs should have been.

Her breath returned, and she remained standing a moment.

The window stood open a few inches, and she stared at the rooftops and traffic below. *Yes, Sophie, you have to do this.* So she set her purse on the sill, safely off the probably dirty floor, then pulled out a tissue and wiped the vinyl seat of a chair facing the bed and sat down.

His whole head was swollen and purplish, with eyes like little holes. A long dark bruise covered his forehead, and a stitched gash coursed from the right temple to the chin. A clear vinyl mask covered his nose and mouth, with a tube running to an oxygen tank. Above that a monitor showed what looked like his heartbeat, with two squiggly lines below. Out of his right arm tubes rose to vinyl bags, one clear, the other blood red. They hung on a pole with a square box that flashed numbers and beeped. His index finger was stuck in a little holder with a wire going to what resembled a smartphone lying next to him. His left arm was missing, the sleeve limp from half way down his upper arm.

Sophie folded her hands in her lap. And kept looking.

Nothing she had ever learned at home or university, nothing she had done in two years at the advertising agency, prepared her for this. *This* did not fit. Anywhere.

Her stomach began to churn.

The middle of the bed. Below his waist. Under the baby blue blanket. Flat.

Oh God, I feel sick. She rose from the chair and clattered her Gucci stilettos into the hallway. "Where's the bathroom?" Her stomach convulsed, and she snatched a tissue from her purse to cover her mouth. A nurse grabbed her other hand, and thrust her into a ladies' room near the elevators.

She vomited into the toilet. Lunch, cocktails, maybe part of breakfast. She knelt down, panting, holding the seat. One last time, just leftover phlegm.

Repulsive.

She crumpled to the floor, sat on it, and leaned against the wall. Her Niemen Marcus dress and Heavenly Delight Skin Care legs. On the tile floor. Next to the toilet. Of the germ-infested, diseased public restroom.

And she sat. Staring at the towel dispenser next to the sink.

She couldn't think of anything to explain the man. But she could no longer think of anything to explain herself either.

Slowly it occurred to her that she didn't care about sitting on the restroom floor. That it had become absurd to care.

Her bruised and bandaged left hand was such a small price that it seemed immoral to only be bruised. The whole thing was wrong. She should have died.

She closed her eyes.

What would cause a man to do such a thing? She had no answer.

So she sat and didn't think about anything.

Tears welled up and kept coming until they streamed down her cheeks. Her chest sporadically contracted and twitched as she cried in gasps and puffs. Some tears dripped off her lips and others found their way down her neck.

The exhaust fan may have muffled her cries to anyone outside. Mercifully no one knocked or turned the door handle.

When Sophie felt strong enough to stand, she struggled to her feet and looked into the mirror. Phlegm dribbled down her chin. She turned on both handles and scooped water to her face—again and again, as if something deep inside her needed washing. A face-full of Christian Dior swirled down the drain.

She looked in the mirror at her plain face, now revealed: no prettier than anyone else's, maybe less. The eyes staring back seemed as if they weren't even hers. And the face didn't seem hers, as if she'd spent her entire young life being someone she wasn't. She shut her eyes and took a deep breath, turned off the water, and paper toweled the remnant of vomit off the toilet seat. She let her hands and face drip and slouched her way back to the room.

A nurse turned away from the monitor and forced a polite smile as she passed.

Sophie went to the window and stared at the traffic below. Wanting to leave, she lifted the handles of her purse and held them briefly. She turned and glanced at the man.

His eyes were open.

She gasped, let go of the purse, and raised her hand to her mouth. Then sat in the chair again.

He turned his head slightly, slowly blinked, and gazed at her from behind the oxygen mask.

Her lower jaw trembled.

Traffic noise drifted through the window.

A voice on the hallway intercom called for someone.

The man stared.

Sophie had graduated *cum laude* from UCLA. Took care to be in all the right circles. And she couldn't think of a thing to say.

The man slowly moved his right hand to the mask and gestured with a feeble flick away from his face.

"Do you . . . Do you want me to take it off?"

He barely nodded.

"The nurses will get mad."

He slightly shook his head and did the flick again.

With a deep breath, and feeling like an accomplice to murder, she pulled the mask below his chin. Couldn't be any worse than what she'd already caused.

"It was you," came his low voice, each word barely audible. "Wasn't it?"

She nodded.

His mouth stretched to what was probably intended as a smile.

She leaned closer with imploring eyes. "I'm—I'm so sorry."

He sighed. His hand pushed toward her, palm up, index finger still wired.

She reached her right hand and hesitantly touched his. The second time in either of their lives they had touched each other. So unlike the first.

"Well then . . . I succeeded."

"You did," she said, almost breathless.

He rasped.

She lifted the mask to his face for a while until he nodded again, and she lowered it back down.

"What is your name?"

"Sophie."

He whispered it to himself.

She pulled the chair closer and leaned on the bed. "Yours is Leonard. You've been all over the news."

He did his attempt at a smile again.

"Why?" She bit her lip and held back the tears. "Why did you do it?"

"Someday you may learn . . . to see beyond yourself."

She cocked her head quizzically.

"That what you have . . . is not important." He closed his eyes. "It's what you give."

In her mind's eye she saw the big yellow truck and the big black tire about to crush her. She closed her eyes and could feel the push. Leonard's push.

She had heard statements like his many times before. Yet this time it wasn't about giving handouts. His gift was beyond explanation.

He nodded, and she understood to raise the mask to his face again and set it in place.

If she agreed with him, she would have to admit that much of her life was a joke. And the fact that she was alive left no choice but to agree.

She glanced at her diamond-studded Lady Rolex— 2:15. A gift to herself, she reasoned when she went into debt for it. Because she deserved it.

No, she didn't. She didn't deserve anything. And she didn't deserve to be alive.

She looked away from him. A Bible and a miniature teddy bear sat on the bedside table. Vases of daisies and roses towered above them.

As the moisture of his breath appeared and disappeared on the inside surface of the mask, she imagined in a steady stream all the things and places and titles she wanted in life. That others told her to get. Or that she had told herself to get. The stream was endless. And as her stream of desires flowed, it seemed to crash on top of itself into a heap.

She would have lost it all, and her life besides, were it not for this wreck who lay in front of her. She didn't even know how to compare her desires to what Leonard had inside him—whatever it was that made him take a crushing tire in her place. Common sense argued back that the heap was still important because everyone said so. But as common as it was, it no longer made sense.

He looked at her, and she took in the image again, especially his eyes, like two little wells on his swollen face.

She and Leonard did not need to talk. Her tears spoke for her. They soon dripped from her chin, and she didn't care where they fell.

He did his smile thing again.

The grinding sound of a truck shifting gears sifted through the window. Then its brakes screeched. Sophie clenched her teeth and reached for his hand, that gift beyond category, and she held it, the most precious thing in her life.

For that brief moment, they were the only two people in the whole world.

His hand feebly squeezed hers.

Movement in the hallway. Voices at the door. She pushed the chair back, grabbed her purse, and scurried past them.

"Isn't that the girl who—"

And she was down the hall to the waiting room.

She sat there all afternoon, peering into the hallway and ignoring the game shows and talk shows that blared for people who didn't want to think about why they were visiting. Whenever a person or group left Leonard's room, she dashed back in just to sit and hold his hand and watch him sleep until voices or footsteps came to the door again.

In the waiting room people entered and left. A mom held a wet towel on her toddler's forehead. A young tattooed man chewed gum, bounced his leg, and stared at the TV, regardless of what was on the screen. A gray-haired man with a face full of stubble closed his eyes and whispered in a foreign language. A woman hunched in the corner whimpered into a cheap, beaten-up cell phone, "How am I going to pay for his bill?"

Sophie wondered at the stories written on each of their faces. And her gaze always drifted back to Leonard's door.

Through the supper hour, no food was brought to his room. A group of people came and did not leave. Nurses and doctors went in and out.

Around 8 p.m. they wheeled out a white body bag that lay flat where the legs should have been.

The group followed silently behind it.

Sophie's breath caught.

Released.

And she screamed. Long, forcefully, from so far down in her gut, that her throat seemed to rip.

Feet and chairs and magazines shuffled around her amid "Oh my God" and "What happened?" The people around Leonard's gurney paused and stared. A plump nurse stepped into the waiting room.

The stretcher and its followers disappeared around the corner by the elevators.

Sophie fell forward off the chair, hit the floor, and wailed. Her whole life ruptured out in sobs. On the beige tiles of the waiting room floor.

She could not stop. Would not. It had to be.

A knee touched the floor beside her, warm hands on her back, and voices spoke in the world beyond her weeping.

She felt herself shuddering then curled onto her knees.

Gradually the cries diminished into sniffling. The flood that had poured out of her slowly dried.

She eventually calmed, and the plump nurse helped her up. "Are you going to be okay, sweetie?"

She nodded, looked into the nurse's gaze, and thought the pupils of her eyes might be some kind of portal to another world. Odd.

The nurse smiled, "Are you sure you're okay?"

"Yeah." She forced a smile. The nurse hugged her and she hugged the nurse back.

Sophie kicked—forced—off her stilettos and shuffled barefoot to the restroom, where she looked into the same mirror. Inside the whites of her own eyes, inside the glistening irises, her pupils peered back and seemed to invite her into some kind of life she had never known. Or one to which she hadn't paid attention. How could she never have paid attention?

Again she took a deep breath in front of the mirror. Then again.

So much to become. So much to do.

She would start now.

With a purpose in her step that felt as new as if she were learning to walk, she marched back to the waiting room. Sat next to the woman with the ratty cell phone. Leaned toward her.

The woman eyed Sophie with a *What-do-you-want?* expression.

"Give me your hand."

The look turned to *Are you crazy?*

Sophie unclipped her watch, pulled the woman's hand, and pressed the watch into her palm, diamonds facing up. "To help pay your bill."

She paused and took in what she had done.

Leonard was right.

And she smiled.

If all the world were blind,
our hearts might see much better.

- 5 -

ANNA'S TREASURES

Seattle 1954

Anna Petrovna died in springtime. She had always wanted to die in winter because that's when everything slept. Death was natural, and properly done, in winter. But the cancer metastasized like a trespasser over the borders of her wishes and took her three seasons early. This upset her.

Sergei clutched her diary as he gazed at the old lithographic photo in the gray light that filtered through the rain-streaked window. By the date on the back, she would have been in her forties, and every inch of her was elegant. Her beauty, high-collared dress, and poise were those of a queen. Two weeks had passed since the funeral. Furniture, appliances, paintings, and clothes had all been sold, given to friends, or delivered to charity. He stood in the empty apartment, its bare white walls bereft of the landscape paintings in baroque frames that once hung on them.

Sergei dropped the photo into the only remaining box of Anna Petrovna's keepsakes. The diary he held was more a record of major life events that skipped through decades. Whether she once had a previous book, he did not know. A lot he did not know. This one started in 1917, and he leafed through it one more time, occasionally struggling with the Old Russian words.

The first entry was dated April 17, 1917: "We moved from Khavarovsk to Vladivostok, where Anatoli makes a great deal of money importing and exporting. We live in a grand home just up the hill from the harbor, bright yellow with broad gables and a balcony. We have a maid, a carriage, fireplaces in four rooms, and more foreign gadgets and ornaments than anyone else in the neighborhood. My favorite is the phonograph from America, on which we listen to rather scratchy renditions of Tchaikovsky and Beethoven."

She made no mention of the Great War. It was thousands of miles away. But under October 1918 she noted, "Red October and the rise of the Bolsheviks" after a reference to a picnic with import-export business owners and their families.

Then May 1919: "The teeth of the Bolsheviks are now sinking into the Far East, and Anatoli and I are classed as bourgeois, which is like being a fire-breathing dragon at Christmas. My sister Karina was hauled out of her home in Khavarovsk, with no word of her after that. To think she's only a day's train ride up the Amur. I so desperately want to look for her, but Anatoli insists it would only make things worse. From hearsay that trickles through the harbor offices, he thinks they'll come for us within weeks or even days. My sister, oh, my sister!"

The next entry, June 1919: "Ocean all around. These are the saddest days of my life. We stole out of our home and boarded a ship bound for Seattle, USA. Anatoli's friends and money secured a place for us, but pulling out of the harbor, I could see our house on the hill, looking like a frightened orphan in the midst of bullies. We hadn't even sold it. Anatoli says we would have been arrested if we had tried, and that the Bolsheviks would have confiscated it anyway. Four miserable trunks are all we have. I am sick from the sea. And sick because of what I have left behind. My house with all its furnishings waits alone on the hill. Into my bag I slipped one phonograph recording to remind me of home. Yet I have faith that when we return, all my things will greet me just as I left them."

September 1919 came several paragraphs below: "I want to go home. The almost constant clouds and rain drive me to despair, and I feel out of place in my mink coat and hat, while others wear thin canvas coats. I can hardly say a word to anyone outside of our small Russian community. I hate the term 'immigrant.' The harbor has no work for Anatoli; he acquired a job as a janitor for a nearby school. How humiliating. We are reduced to living in a dingy, two-room, red-brick apartment above a noisy street."

Sergei turned a few pages. January 1921: "Anatoli insists that we cannot go home. Lenin is in firm control of the whole country. We may as well try to be American. My home, my furniture, my phonograph recordings. How are they now?" The April entry read: "Good news! Anatoli has improved his English enough to secure a job at the harbor. Life will improve again."

Then Sergei found March 1922: "We have adopted an orphaned boy. He is the son of newly arrived refugees from St. Petersburg, who were Protestants. They fell ill and died of typhoid, but the boy was quarantined and saved. His name is Sergei and he is eight. He is a mild, fearful boy, but surviving the loss of his parents and the un-Russian beliefs they held, that is understandable. I am pleased to possess a child without the disgusting ordeal of childbirth. We are now a proper family."

Sergei reread it—"possess a child." He imagined himself as a marble statue, standing next to her furniture. Whatever he thought or did, he always had to look good.

The tear trickling down his cheek imitated the drops on the window. Death had wrenched from his hands the birth mother he loved. Almost as bad, he couldn't remember what she looked like. And someone between her and the adoption agency had destroyed her photo. At least the mother who raised him seemed to think of him as a good possession.

He leafed through a few years to November 1926: "The happiest day of my life came last week! We moved into a white house with a picture window and a broad porch around the front door. My life has returned. I can be respected again. Anatoli has done well and proved himself a good husband. French provincial furniture is what I want more than anything." He never remembered any furniture besides the stuffed sofa and straight-legged chairs and tables. But he remembered playing on the big porch. It was great for a tricycle and rubber ball.

Sergei skipped ahead to September 1928: "Sergei begins high school today. What an admirable young man he has become. He is bilingual, a mediocre sportsman, but a fine academic. He is intelligent and always seems to be thinking something. I trust he will make a lot of money someday." Yes, that was why she recited his good grades to everyone she knew.

He turned two pages to November 1929: "The news is bad these days. I had always thought depression was something *I* felt when things were bad. It seems the whole of America will be dragged into poverty. I hope it doesn't interfere with the Ladies' Club. I'm concerned for Anatoli. How can he do well in such circumstances?"

Sergei skimmed the entries of how difficult house payments became, to where the house was foreclosed, and the family moved back into an apartment. He remembered the silence at the supper table. But he had never understood why Mother spent so many hours crying in her bedroom. Father usually stared out the window. His hands, so used to working, could only fidget.

Sergei had met someone about that time, a man distributing pamphlets on a street corner who offered hope beyond the economic collapse. The man taught him that God was not a Russian, and life was more than owning a house. Sergei wondered if the things he came to believe, the new life he experienced, were like those of his birth mother and father. His father Anatoli had nodded his approval, but Anna Petrovna only said, "Think of the house we lost!"

Yet they never had to stand in food lines.

Sergei paged past the years where she noted his entry into the University of Washington with money Anatoli had hidden away. On another page Sergei had taken a position as a high school teacher. Later on he married Nina, "a lovely, respectable young lady." On another page came the first grandchild, Anton, "a nuisance if there ever was one, but nevertheless a happy child and a guarantee to the family line." That was when Father's long-lost smile returned, and Mother carried the baby pictures everywhere. Little Anton was the one thing that he and his mother cherished with equal passion, and he smiled at the singular thought.

Father's cardiac arrest must have been too painful for her to record. She only noted the date of the funeral then the "darkness and emptiness" that closed around her. The journal held only two undated entries after that—the cancer diagnosis and a final, pathetic wish to return to her house on the hill in Vladivostok.

He bit his lip over a trembling breath. Even if she'd gotten her wish, she'd have been disappointed at what would have become of the old house after all these years. Most likely it would have been ransacked and looted. Maybe taken over by a Communist party official, complete with a Joseph Stalin portrait hanging on the wall.

His chest tightened. All that had happened to her. All that had eluded her grasp. A disgust that often lingered on the fringes of his thoughts finally flared up. And he shouted, "You had so many chances to wake up!"

Loving her had been like loving a mannequin.

He knew it was futile, but he wondered, as he often had, if he could have tried harder. And each piece of his fragmented heart weighed more than the whole should have.

He closed the diary and dropped it into the cardboard box. As it plopped, it displaced the photos to reveal the one phonograph record that Anna Petrovna had brought from Russia and played a thousand times to shut out the world into which she had been sentenced. She played it more than any of those she had bought in America. His teeth clenched. He picked it up. It was scratched and pockmarked, and its faded label read "P. I. Tchaikovsky, *The Nutcracker*." He had heard it over and over—and could still see his mother dancing in circles by herself as it played. Though he liked the music, it was all about a dream, a dream that drugged her from the ability to enjoy anything real.

He held the record on one palm and with his other hand pressed his fingernails into the black vinyl. He pulled them across the grooves to make the deepest scratches the vintage disc had ever sustained.

Sorry, Mother.

He bit his lip.

No, I'm not.

With both hands he gripped it. Flexed it.

Broke it in half.

He cracked it into quarters; several fragments splintered and fell at his feet. He stared at the pieces in his hand. Then hurled them across the room. They clattered against a wall and littered the floor.

The air hung still, like a silent requiem to these last bits of her deterrents to life.

The door creaked open. Nina and Anton stepped in. She held their son's hand and embraced Sergei. "What's wrong?"

"Everything."

Silence.

"No. Nothing."

She looked at him quizzically.

"If a person's life was empty, how can anything be left? So there's nothing to be wrong anymore."

The cloud-muted light diffused through the window to the paint-chipped windowsills, the uneven floorboards, the adjoining bedroom and kitchen. Here he had spent his last two years of high school and all his college years. Here his father had died. And from here his mother had never moved back to a real house. But the roof had kept them dry. The windows had let in the light. The table rarely lacked food. And they had each other. The room did not demand despair from anyone, except of course from Anna Petrovna.

"Hmmm. How did we miss that junk?" Nina walked to the wall, and Anton helped her pick up the broken record pieces.

Junk.

She looked around the room.

"I took out the waste bin," Sergei said. "Toss them in the box."

She dropped the splinters on top of the diary and noticed the fragments at his feet. "Aha." She scrutinized him, but he kept staring at the window. She nodded some kind of understanding, picked up the pieces, and touched his hand. "Are you ready to go?"

"I loved her anyway. Did I try hard enough?"

She exhaled loudly. "Visited every week and listened to her lament. Shopped for her and did all her business. Hugged her and prayed for her. Do you want me to keep going?"

He held up his hand to say *enough*.

The rain streaks on the window were the last rinse of anything in that apartment that might have lingered.

He crouched and lifted the box. A cardboard box. With photos, a diary, and splinters of a record. All that remained from the world of Anna Petrovna.

Their footsteps echoed in the hollow room as they shuffled out. And the room's last anguish was the simple click of the shutting door.

The one who gives away ends up with the most.

- 6 -

BRONZE MAN

"These are the words of the Son of God,
whose eyes are like blazing fire and whose feet
are like burnished bronze" (Revelation 2:9).

"Make a horn at each of the four corners,
so that the horns and the altar are of one piece,
and overlay the altar with bronze" (Exodus 27:2).

"Offer your bodies as living sacrifices . . ."
(Romans 12:1).

In late afternoon I met a woman in a park. She sat in a circle of elementary school kids, doing crafts with Popsicle sticks and telling stories about what's important in life. I paused to watch, and she called me over to help.

She said I looked as if I needed to join in as much as the kids.

Not sure how or why to say no, I sat down with them. I listened and helped. I asked her why she did this, and she said, "It's an expression of my faith."

"Oh."

Now as I lay in bed, I still felt the odd happiness that coursed through me when I helped the kids glue Popsicle sticks together and listened to the woman's stories. And I felt bothered because I couldn't escape how right she was—that I needed to join her.

Finally I drifted into sleep, and perhaps a dream. . . .

I found myself walking on a city sidewalk.

From a horde of sweat-drenched bodies bustling through a cavern of concrete, glass, and steel, a man emerged and stood at a street corner. Signal lights traded red, green, and yellow, while trucks ground by and cars weaved around them.

The man's skin was not so much dark as it was bronzed, otherworldly, like a living statue. Yet he wore blue jeans and a white shirt. Several people met his gaze and did double takes. His eyes were luminescent and unsettling. I couldn't help but follow him.

He walked to the city hall, where men and women in dark suits and dresses marched up and down a hillside of steps, past pillars and heavy doors. They carried briefcases, checked their watches, and held cellphones to their ears. The Bronze Man turned away. He walked through the financial district, stopped briefly under the towers of glass and concrete, and went on. He passed through the garment and electronics districts. When he would not buy, sellers turned toward the next passerby. He ventured into places not marked on the map, where people lived in cardboard boxes and others carried guns and sold bags of white powder. The Bronze Man shook his head and kept walking.

He stopped in a trash-filled park then raised his hands and his voice. "This land was once a vast forest, but this city you have built on it now subjugates your souls. I am here to heal this place and to save you from yourselves."

People stopped. "Where did he come from?"

He raised his hands again: "Turn around! The city is to be changed. Come, follow me."

The people stared. "Weirdo."

The Bronze Man turned and continued walking through the city. Some people returned to their shopping and their business. A few kept staring. Others followed with me just to see what he would do next.

As he walked, the followers increased to a small crowd.

"To change a city," he said, "we need hands to work. Give me your hands!"

"What will you give us?" they asked.

"A new city."

"Pffft! Yeah, right."

"Who will give me their hands?" asked the Bronze Man.

"I need both hands to work." "I need both hands to sail my yacht."

"Is anyone willing to give me their hands?"

"I will." A voice rose from the back of the crowd as a young woman emerged. She held a toddler in one arm and clutched an older one with the other. "Without hands I can still survive. Though I must cook and clean, my children and husband will help."

Like lightning, the Bronze Man thrust his hand at her, and in the blinding flash both her hands were gone. I gasped, along with the crowd, as she tottered from the shock. No blood or gore, her hands simply disappeared. At first bewildered, she looked at the clean stumps at the ends of her arms, then the look in her eyes turned to resolve. With the toddler still in one arm and the older child holding the other, she followed behind the Bronze Man.

What kind of person is this? I wondered.

"To change a city," he said, "we need feet to travel. Give me your feet."

"What will you give us?"

"A new city."

"Give me a break." "Duh! I need both feet to walk." "You ain't cutting off my feet!"

"Who is willing to give me their feet?" asked the Bronze Man.

"I will," called a voice from the edge of the spectators. An elderly man stepped forward. "I love to walk early each morning and hike in the countryside. But I've hiked enough. I'm content to sit and enjoy the world from a chair."

In a flash the Bronze Man thrust his hand and seized the man's feet. He jerked and fell awkwardly to the ground. Like the woman's hands, the man's feet vanished the instant the Bronze Man grasped them. The woman whose hands had just been taken set her toddler down to walk with the older child then reached her free arm toward the elderly man. He took hold of her, and she supported him as he stumbled along next to her children following the Bronze Man.

Where is he going? I wondered.

"To change a city, we need eyes to see."

"Oh yeah? And what will you give us this time?"

"A new city."

"Are you crazy?" "You sound like a cult leader to me." "Get him out of here!"

"Who will give me their eyes?"

I hoped he wouldn't call on me. But the way others seemed to not notice me, and even look through me, I may have been invisible to them.

Then to my relief a young man stepped up. "I will. I'm a university student. I often study long into the night. But I've learned enough from books and am ready to learn from darkness."

Again the blazing flash, and the man's eyes were gone. His head quivered, and the crowd gasped at the empty sockets in his face. The man whose feet had disappeared held onto the young mother with one hand and took the hand of the blind young man with the other.

"To change a city, we need mouths to speak."

"And you'll give us a new city?"

"Yes. A new city."

"He says that every time. Liar!" "We wouldn't be able to speak one word to each other." "You're insane."

"Who will give me their mouth?"

A woman came from the side. She was middle-aged, slightly grayed, and carried herself with dignity. "I'm a teacher. I've spoken to my students countless hours over many years. But from now on, I will use only the chalk or marker in my hand."

In a flash the Bronze Man wiped out her mouth. The impact spun her in a circle. The blind student reached his hand in her direction until she steadied herself and caught it.

They walked on.

It appeared to me that the Bronze Man was leading them in a loop around the city.

"To change a city, we need ears to hear."

"For what? You won't give us anything."

"I will. A new city."

"That's enough!" "Are you trafficking in body parts?"

"Who will give me their ears?"

"I believe I must," said a woman standing before him. "I'm a guitarist and a composer. I've sold records and have performances scheduled for the next three years. But I will rely on what I can play and sing by memory and hope the sounds come out right."

The flash again, and both her ears disappeared. She arched back and spread her arms to keep her balance. The teacher grabbed her hand and hugged her.

"To change a city, we need minds to think."

"Now you've gone too far, Bronze Man!" "Yeah, if we give you our minds, you'll control us." "And for this you'll promise us a new city?"

"Yes. You have said it."

"No way!" "You can't change the city. You're only exploiting us!"

"Who will give me their mind?"

Silence came over the crowd until a man stepped forward, one who had passed by the Bronze Man in the financial district. Still in his blue pinstriped suit and wingtip shoes, he looked less confident than before. He set his briefcase down. "I own a stock brokerage, land, and shares in the largest corporations in the region. Making the right decisions quickly is essential to everything I do. But perhaps I've earned enough. If I've made any friends, I'll trust them to help me from now on."

A roaring flash sent the crowd cowering as the Bronze Man pierced the man's head. He reeled and stumbled in a daze. When the air settled, the musician picked up the businessman's briefcase and held his arm.

This was too much. I could not even think of what to say.

The Bronze Man walked along with his maimed and hobbling followers. The surrounding crowd grew larger. He stopped.

"To change a city we must have hearts to care."

"Go away, Bronze Man! You're a deceiver." "He's going to take everything we have." "This guy's dangerous. Somebody call the police." Voices shouted over other voices in a cacophonous roar, denouncing him and ridiculing those who followed.

The Bronze Man and his followers stood still until the crowd calmed. Yet faces remained tense.

"What will you give us?" now came as a taunt, not a question.

"A new city."

"Liar!" "It's impossible!" "You're a criminal!"

At the top of his voice the Bronze Man shouted, "Who . . . will give me . . . their heart?"

The crowd hushed: fear, expectation, curiosity all at once.

"You've got to be kidding," a voice snickered as a short, stout figure came to the front. "He ain't got a heart." The volunteer appeared fatigued and was dirty from head to foot in worn-out clothes, with missing teeth and hair cropped haphazardly. Ashamed even to look at the Bronze Man, he kept his head bowed. He opened his mouth but was apparently too embarrassed to speak.

"Go home and take a bath!" Laughter rippled through the crowd. The short, stout slob swayed one way and then the other in fright. He turned to slither back into the crowd, humiliated that he had been so presumptuous.

"Stop," the Bronze Man said.

He stopped.

"Speak."

"I . . . I'm a day laborer. I got no education, no money, no skill. I live on the street. I don't know how much of a heart I've got left after the life I've lived." He broke off and only shook his head. "But if you still want my heart, it's yours."

The blinding flash. Those in the front of the crowd toppled back as the Bronze Man pierced the man's chest. He jolted backward and crumpled to the ground. The businessman, still in a daze, steadied his hand on the day laborer, paused, then lifted the man by the arm and held him until he could stand. The day laborer shuffled haltingly to the mother and set his hand on her shoulder beside the baby.

The crowd stood silent. I stood silent.

The Bronze Man looked on his seven followers and smiled. A tear formed in his eye and grew until it trickled down his cheeks. They had made a circle, with him in the center.

He surveyed the crowd. Again he wept, but without a smile.

Eyes back on his followers, his smile returned through the tears. "It is enough." One-by-one he touched them and whispered a blessing. Then he kept walking.

As they walked away, I was lifted up, floating in air. And I continued to watch as they followed him.

Hobbling in their circle around him, they did not say or ask anything. On through the day they walked, slowly, diligently, around the city. They did not argue. They did not suggest.

Then the group seemed to reproduce itself into two, then four, then eight, until I lost count. And all across the city, each group was different from the others and did what each of their people was inclined to do.

The oddest thing about this group and all its multiplications was what looked like the same bronze-colored man. He was always at the center and appeared most important to them. It was odd because he had no hands, no feet, no eyes, no mouth, no ears, and both his head and chest were pierced open. Yet a power seemed to emanate from this man—all the people got their energy from him. And their hands, feet, eyes, mouths, ears, heads, and hearts were intact and vibrant with life.

A closer look revealed that the Bronze Man was not physically there at all. He had entered into each of his followers, and they were all becoming bronze.

***

Then I awoke.

I wondered. And I grew perplexed.

I considered my own body parts. I imagined how the Bronze Man had changed those people, had lived in their lives—and how he might change and live in mine.

I could still see myself with the woman and the kids in the park. And I suspected my dream was more than that.

Throughout the week I scoured newspapers, blogs, television news, online neighborhood news, and I did a lot of asking around.

One-by-one I found them, the ones who had followed in the dream. The easiest was the headline news of the businessman who masterminded and financed unprecedented projects.

Through word of mouth I met the day laborer who poured out so much love that the hardest hearts on skid row cracked open and shared the same love with others.

I went to the cathedral and heard the musician who played stirring melodies, melting the hearts of those who heard.

Then I attended a rally where the teacher who captivated audiences with her speeches inspired others to help change the city.

I read a magazine article about the university student who, with an eagle eye, uncovered corruption in the city.

I walked with the old man who tirelessly trudged from home to home to learn people's needs and connect them with those who could assist.

And the woman with two kids—the first one in the dream, who had given her hands—I found her in the park with her toddler and her older child, telling stories about what was important in life and doing crafts with the kids, this time using finger paint to make cheerful posters for nursing homes.

I sat down and rolled up my sleeves. Tears welled in my eyes.

She smiled and said, "Welcome back."

The best thing you could possibly have
is a hunger for God
because you'll always get more of him.

- 7 -

THE WONDER OF OG

Og traced his fingers across the images of sun and moon he had scratched on his cave wall. His father had taught him to bow down to the sun each morning and the moon each night. They ruled the sky, and every day and night they crossed from one end to the other. Bowing to them made sense, even if they sometimes hid behind the white fields that floated in the sky.

Yet Og could not stop wondering if there might be something beyond the sun and moon. They were gods of the sky, but how did they get there?

He stepped past his woman, Enu, with Little Og on her back, as she cooked meat on a stick over the fire, and he looked across the valley that spread beyond his cave. *Why do I ask these things?*

He did not know. No one else asked such things, so they could not help him.

Stories of the first people had long been told around fires at night, like stories of the first man and woman who lived in a big garden, and of a young man who killed his own brother. Other stories were of hunting big animals and crossing big fields of water where the land was so far away it could not be seen.

Og's father and mother had taught him all the stories, and they had heard them from their own parents, who in turn had heard them from theirs. But no one knew where the stories started.

It was said that the first people were made by a great God. Out of dirt. The first people talked to this God, and the God talked back. But they also made the great God mad and had to leave the garden. So it was said.

Og wanted to talk to this God too. But he did not know where the garden was, or if the God had also left the garden. He wanted to know where the God lived. And he wanted to ask if this great God had made the sun and the moon because they ruled the day and the night but did not seem to make anything the way the great God did.

The others across the valley said he was crazy. Everyone knew enough to worship the gods of the sky and of the mountains, streams, forests, and fields. "Just believe. Do not be different," they would say. They often shook their heads at him. "There are no answers to your questions."

But Og could not help but wonder if this great God were above everything they saw. If he could talk to this God the way some did in the stories, he might find out. And he wondered what it would be like to bow to only one God.

"Og, eat." Enu pulled the meat from the fire and set baskets of fruits and nuts on a straw mat.

He smiled at her and sat on his rock.

She set Little Og on the ground, and he reached for the berries. Whatever he ate, he pushed into his mouth with a flat hand, so his face was always dirty with whatever did not go in.

Og asked Enu if she thought the great God liked to sing. The birds sang all day, and each one was different. What did they sing about? Were they singing to the great God? Or did the great God sing through them to Og?

"I do not know." Enu smiled and shook her head. Then she made up a song about how she loved him and Little Og.

He smiled and held her close.

Then he told her one of the stories about how people became very bad and the great God sent a big flood to kill everyone, except for the animals and a faithful man and his family who started life over for everyone.

Og wished he could have met this man and wondered how many parents before him this man lived.

Enu held him and said, "You would have done the same as that faithful man."

After Little Og fell asleep on the animal skin bed, and as the fire died down, Enu leaned close to Og. "Do the stars each have stories?" she asked.

"They must. We have not heard them yet."

She moved her hand across his back and around his neck. Then she put her lips to his.

Og liked it. And he wondered why he had such feelings when she did that. He wondered why he tingled so much when he joined himself to her. And he wondered how out of her inside came Little Og. How was a child created in her body?

Perhaps the great God, or some god, would make Enu's belly grow large again. They would have another Little Og. Or maybe a Little Enu.

What is this wonder between a man and a woman? he thought as he touched her face.

***

The next morning Og took his bow, arrows, knife, and spear to go hunting.

Enu pointed to a new place where she would climb to look for fruit and roots. She touched her lips to his.

Og came to a stream at the bottom of the valley. He stopped and sat on a rock.

It was the same rock where several seasons before he had been washing blood from a deer he had hunted. Another man had appeared, one he did not know and who did not smile.

Og relived the day inside his head, and he felt bad—like the way he had felt then. The man had grabbed the deer out of Og's hands and pushed him away, but Og knew that every man must hunt his own food, so he grabbed it back. The man pushed Og over the same rock he now sat on, and the man took Og's own spear and lifted it to kill him, but Og pushed the man back, and his head hit the rock and he lay still.

Og felt afraid the man would wake up and try to kill him again, or find Enu and Little Og and take them away. So he dragged the man into the water and held the head down for a long time.

When the body grew cold, he dragged it far into the forest and covered it with branches. He did not want to eat it. He did not want to drag it home with the deer either. Eating another man was said to be wrong, different from eating an animal. But he did not know why.

More than that he felt bad that he had killed the man. His heart felt dark like the night and hard like a rock.

When he thanked the spirit of an animal he had killed to eat, he only felt a little bad. Then he felt happy when he ate. But when he killed the man, even though the man had tried to kill him, he felt very bad. And he still felt bad today. But he did not know why.

The spirit of a human was different from that of an animal. Where did the life inside the man go after he died? Did it go somewhere no one could see?

Og sat on the rock a long time.

***

As the sun was finishing its journey across the sky that day, Og shot two arrows into a deer and followed it until it fell and stopped breathing. After thanking the animal's spirit, he cut two branches with leaves, tied them together with a piece of rope, laid the deer on it, and dragged it toward home.

At the river he cut the deer open and cleaned it out. He found himself looking up again and again in case another man came.

He grunted and pulled the deer up the hill to his cave.

Enu would be proud of him. And that would make him happy and want to hunt again.

They would be busy for many days, cutting meat and hanging it to dry, cooking over the fire, and eating until their stomachs hurt.

He called out when he reached the cave. But Enu did not greet him. He heard only a groan from inside.

There lay Enu and Little Og. Their faces were a strange color, like the color of some of the flowers or of the sky in early evening. This was very bad.

She could hardly talk, and Little Og was not breathing. A basket of berries he had never seen before lay in the middle of the cave.

He screamed and kicked the basket out of the cave.

Enu smiled weakly and tried to lift her hand to him. But it barely moved. He held her hand, but it did not squeeze his hand in return the way it normally did. He looked into her eyes and could see that they had lost their life. "No!" he pleaded. "Life, come back to Enu!" He sat and pulled her and Little Og tight to his own body. Perhaps the life in him could help the life in each of them. Even if his life left him, he wanted them to live.

But Little Og was growing cold, and Enu's weak smile disappeared.

Kneeling over them, his body shook as tears fell from his eyes. He felt he had no courage, no strength—lost and afraid, the way he had once been as a child when wandering in the forest apart from his father. He was afraid of being alone. His strength meant nothing without Enu. And tomorrow was useless without Little Og.

When the sun disappeared across the valley, Og put his lips to hers and knew it would be the last time.

As the moon rose in the sky, Enu stopped breathing, and her body slowly grew cold.

Og cried and cried.

All night he could not sleep. He touched their bodies and wandered in circles in front of the cave. Where did the life inside them go? To the same place of the bad man at the river? Or to another place, a place better than the land where they lived?

Before the sun took over the sky, he slept only because he was so tired.

***

The birds woke him. But he did not want to hear their songs anymore. He wanted only to hear what the great God had to say about all this. And he wanted to know where the lives of Enu and Little Og went.

Og looked around his cave. The pictures of the sun and moon seemed useless to him. Everything was useless. How could he feel such pain inside of him when he had no outward wounds?

Og lay on top of Enu and Little Og. He wanted to die too and go where their spirits went. But he was afraid to kill himself. And he did not know why.

The pain inside him would not go away. And he did not want to eat the deer he had killed. He did not want to eat anything.

He carried Enu and Little Og, one at a time, far into the forest. He cried as he carried each one, laid them next to each other, then covered them with branches. He sat next to them until the sun rose high.

Did the great God know they died? Did the great God care? Did the great God know how terrible Og felt?

Og had to find out.

More than that he had to finally meet the great God.

He returned to his cave, but it was a place of tears without Enu or Little Og. He heard their voices in his head but not through his ears. His body crumpled to the dirt and lay there as if he had been beaten with a club, and he knew he could not live there anymore.

He decided to leave the cave and never go back. He wrapped himself in his animal skins, took one extra, and put all his dried meat into a pouch. Spear in hand, he started walking toward the sun.

But the sun stayed ahead of him until it went to sleep behind the distant land. He did not want to chase the moon, so he curled into his animal skins and slept.

***

The next morning Og started after the sun again, but when the sun was high, he stopped and thought. The sun would continue its same journey across the sky as it always did. It would not stop to meet him.

And as he thought, he looked at a mountain before him. It rose into the white fields of the sky. Higher than anything else there was.

That is where he would find the great God. If that God could be found.

He walked two days, finishing the meat and eating berries and roots along the way, but not the berries Enu and Little Og had eaten.

On the second day the mountain rose gently then steeper the farther up he went. The air got much colder, and he wondered why. He climbed higher than he had ever known a man could climb.

From the mountain the land below looked far away, and he had never known there was so much of it. He wondered how far it went, and as the sun traded places with the moon, he curled in the fur of his extra animal skin and slept between two rocks.

The next day Og kept climbing and reached the white fields of the sky. He did not know a man could walk in them, so high up. They floated like smoke but did not hurt his eyes. They were cold and wet against his face. Then the wind blew them away, and he saw the sun.

Even in the sun the air grew colder than it had ever felt, even during the cold season. And he could no longer breathe very well, but he kept climbing, and the spear made a good walking stick.

After a while the trees disappeared, then the bushes, until there was only rock. He wondered why and thought, *I must be getting closer to this God.* As the sky darkened, he found a hollow place in the side of the mountain and piled rocks to make a wall that would keep out the wind. Yet even in his extra animal skin, he shivered most of the night.

As the sun rose, Og wondered how he could be above the floating white fields even though he was on land. He started climbing again and kept the animal skin wrapped tight, cut off a piece, and tied it over the old pieces around his feet.

Farther up, the mountainside was covered in something like white sand. The white stuff was very cold. It looked like ground, but it broke under his feet like powder, like air itself. He had never seen anything so strange.

The great God must live here.

But no matter how high he climbed, the sun was still higher, and late in the day it only moved away from him.

He hoped he had made the right decision about where to find the great God. He stopped to rest and think about it, and decided that because the sun was so small and the mountain so big, this God must live on the mountain and had spread the white stuff as a sign.

So he kept climbing, even though he could hardly breathe.

At the end of the day, he watched the sun sink below the floating white fields. He was now sure he would meet the great God here, and nothing would stop him.

His legs ached and wanted to stop, but he refused to listen to them and forced one foot forward, then the other, until the mountain did not go up any more. It became flat then went down in every direction. He had reached the top.

As he stopped, he began to shiver. He pulled the animal skins tighter, but could not stop shaking.

Now I will meet this great God.

Og dropped his spear and knelt on both knees. The white stuff felt so cold. He lay the extra animal skin below his knees and they felt warm again.

He raised his arms the way one might if carrying a bundle of sticks.

The wind swept through his hair and bit as if an animal gnawed his flesh.

He held his position for a long time.

Something seemed to surround him, a presence like he had never felt before. Yet he was alone with white specks swirling in the air around him. Maybe the presence was in the white specks.

His chest thumped harder. The presence seemed to make him lift his arms higher and wider, as if to embrace this God.

He had not known that the great God lived in such a cold place. Og's body shivered violently, and his teeth clattered. But he would not let this God go.

His arms ached and wanted to rest. No. He would not give up.

He could not feel his legs anymore. He could not feel his hands, and his shoulders felt only pain. But he kept his hands raised.

"Come to meee!" he bellowed.

The presence grew stronger. With a tingling it seemed to hold his arms.

He was not imagining, or dreaming, or wishing.

Then he no longer felt cold. Nor warm. Just the presence.

The great God seemed to say, *I am here*. And without words, Og understood. His questions seemed answered without being asked.

He did not want to move, even after the sky turned dark, and the stars hung brighter than he had ever seen.

His chest grew still, until he hardly breathed. And his arms seemed to hold themselves up. Every part of his body was stiff.

But that was fine. He had found what he had always looked for. And more.

All was well.

***

For thousands of years on top of that mountain there knelt a frozen figure in animal skins with arms outstretched and head looking up.

The three mountain climbers who found this wonder grinned and chattered on morning talk shows, scientific conferences, and university presentations.

They said that warming temperatures had thawed the ice enough for the body to be visible. And perfectly intact.

But they did not know where the man had come from.

Or why he climbed the mountain.

Or how he could possibly have frozen to death with arms raised.

Or why.

Why on earth would a person do that?

Og knows.

Just when we thought we had reached a wall,
we walked through a door.

- 8 -

JOURNEY TO THE EDGE

Suited up, helmets on, inside the spacecraft Wilson and Clark climbed into their seats. Switches, dials, and levers filled every inch of the surrounding control panels. Gauges and monitors glowed in green and amber, a soft visual buffer to the darkness outside.

Wilson glanced at the small mirror he'd glued—against regulations—to the console. No sandy brown hair and gray-blue eyes looking back, just the white sphere of his helmet and the face shield that looked like the giant eye of a bug. A bug in outer space. Just how he felt.

We've traveled so far, so long, beyond time. What is this in front of us?

Wilson and Clark were approaching a massive surface—maybe the edge of the Universe, or the edge of something. He fastened his buckles.

The necessities of recycling oxygen, water, and waste, and especially of growing food, limited the spacecraft to two astronauts hurtling through empty space, light-years alone. When Wilson didn't feel like a bug, he felt as if he and Clark were the sum of all of humanity.

So on behalf of The World Space Authority, they sought answers to the big questions: Did the Universe have an edge? And what, if anything, was beyond it? Or would electromagnetic forces arc them back from it? If the Universe were expanding, would its edge always be ahead of them? The God question was never an official subject, but it lingered behind the science. Early on Wilson thought he might find some evidence of God out here. But no sign. At first it confirmed his skepticism. Then he wondered if the whole thing were an immense divine expression. He had always thought most religions kept their renditions of God inside their buildings. Maybe the Universe was God's church. But where the heck was *he*?

Whenever Wilson considered the big questions, he eventually came back to the more practical question: Would he and Clark ever return to Earth? And if they did, would the human race still be in business?

The wall was getting closer. He took a deep breath.

Wilson and Clark, like most of humanity, didn't like mysteries they couldn't solve. So they'd come this far, and would go much farther, in their pursuit of answers.

Clark flipped switches and scanned dials. Through the intercom he said, "Internal systems normal."

For now anyway.

Before them loomed the biggest mystery to date. Readings indicated that in this barrier, they had found the long-theorized Einstein-Rosen Bridge—a wormhole. Hopefully it would be the Morris-Thorne version and let them return from the other direction.

They could feel the ship being pulled toward the massive plane of light streaks that converged into a wide circle sloping into a funnel.

"Wilson, look at this. And this."

Wilson leaned toward a pair of meters. One indicated increasing fields of electromagnetism. They'd expected that, and it would surely increase. The other one indicated rising levels of radiation. Wilson swallowed hard. They'd expected that too. He could hear himself breathing.

Clark did not look at him but glanced outside then back to the two meters with lights climbing slowly from yellow to orange.

"Deploy virtual lead shields."

"Deploying." Clark reached down and yanked a switch. Outside came a *vooooom*, followed by loud humming of the activators.

So far the stabilizing thrusters worked, but there was no pulling out of the wormhole's gravitational force.

They had no guarantee of the wormhole's stability, or whether or not it would collapse and annihilate them. Wilson's nerves started to fray. Clark appeared calm, probably too focused on the controls to think about himself. He adjusted the stabilizers. "Velocity increasing. Structural integrity stable."

The light streaks grew brighter. The pull gradually and steadily surged, drawing them toward what appeared to be the outer rim of the wormhole.

The two monitors rose to orange.

The most sophisticated space mission in Earth's history. And now in this moment, we have no control and no idea what'll happen.

The ship began to curve in a wide circle around the wormhole's opening. The ride was smooth but gaining speed. Their arc gradually tightened—like those wishing well coin funnels at shopping malls, where one would release a coin through a slot and watch it spiral around until it disappeared down the center.

They descended lower, faster, until they corkscrewed into the hole.

The two monitors flashed red.

Wilson's heart jackhammered.

None of the simulations they had performed back on Earth could have prepared them to be sucked into this electromagnetic vortex.

The rising g-force and centrifugal force—it was hard to distinguish—pressed into him like a hand squeezing him against his seat. He could no longer lift his arms. Or move any part of his body. The squeeze increased, pressing the air out of his lungs. He gasped.

The ship started to quiver. Then shake.

A slow twist, then the ship lurched in a blinding spin. Whirling and whirling. Wilson felt as if he were in the spin cycle of a washing machine. He grew immediately nauseated, a sharp pain in his head, then slipped into a stunned daze. Everything turned gray, then darkened until he lost consciousness, and there was nothing.

***

The dead void turned to haze, peaceful and still. It gave way to sunshine, and Wilson saw himself in a forest of pine trees. He was a boy, maybe fourteen years old. He looked up and marveled at the glistening white auras around each pine needle swaying in the light.

"There's one, Son." His father stepped beside him and pointed to the left. Poking through the carpet of brown needles between two large tree trunks, rising like a lone, defiant miniature princess, bloomed an orchid.

Wilson gazed at its white petals spread like wings above a pink slipper and yellow stamens. He'd previously seen photos but never the real thing. Though other boys might have thought him strange, a sense rushed through him that he'd just discovered a treasure.

The scene froze in time and space, still, as if set apart for eternity. Just the elegant flower and the shimmering pine needles.

"What's the matter?" came his father's voice.

Wonder. Young Wilson was enrapt between the wonder above him and the one below.

Then he felt the breeze that had been blowing all along, cool and fresh, as if coming from heaven itself.

Beside his father he walked reverently toward the orchid, knelt, and leaned close. Veins traversed the petals like the blood vessels in his own arms. The slipper part was perfectly formed, as if preordained to cuddle a fairy. Even the two broad, pointed leaves, translucent in the sun, burgeoned with a life force.

Kneeling beside his father, it seemed to Wilson that the entire Universe in its grandiosity and its intimacy revealed itself in the glowing pine needles and the flower.

As he considered this, he looked at his own hands, his body, and he felt as if he were looking at himself from outside. Whether or not in a body, his heart and mind—all on their own—looked out in the middle of this Universe. It wasn't like any awareness as when he walked to school or played basketball or studied. And it went beyond any elation he felt when he gazed at a pretty girl he liked. It was as if God himself had pulled back a curtain and, through the simple beauties of nature, smiled and drew Wilson to the edge of himself, beyond questions to where no words were spoken. To where earth and heaven met.

He reached up.

The haze drifted back over him.

***

Nothing. Black and empty. A growing sense of motion.

Spinning. Like the inside rim of a wheel, endlessly spinning. Like a dream from which Wilson could not awake.

Slowly the nothingness cleared. He thought he was opening his eyes, but he wasn't sure. Everything was black.

And all was silent. No engine sound or control panel beeps.

Still spinning.

Then he could see distant starlight twirling outside the windshield. He was back in space. Inside his suit. Helmet on.

The control panels were all dark.

As he regained his senses, he fumbled until he found the starboard horizontal stabilizer. He pulled it. Nothing.

What?

Then he remembered. Red lights on the monitors. The electromagnetic field of the wormhole must have shut down the spacecraft's electrical systems.

He could still breathe inside the space suit.

Still dizzy, he unbuckled himself and struggled out of his seat. The centrifugal force of the spinning pressed him against the ceiling.

Clark was still unconscious.

Careful not to flip any switches, Wilson inched himself along the ceiling of the cabin back to the master electrical panel. Working by feel and familiarity with where things were, he shut down the master electrical lever. He couldn't see the main fuses but by touch could sense they'd all been thrown. He heaved the master lever back on then one-by-one flipped on the fuses.

Lights flickered throughout the cabin. Good sign.

He could only hope that the virtual lead shields had remained on long enough to save Clark and him from the high radiation. Time would reveal that answer.

The ship still spinning, Wilson pulled himself back to his seat and activated the horizontal stabilizer until the motion stopped. He adjusted cabin oxygen levels then removed his helmet, lay back, and remained still until the nausea, dizziness, and headache subsided.

Clark stirred, looked at him, and removed his helmet. "What was that?"

Wilson chuckled. "A ride. We're on the other side."

"The wormhole."

"Yup."

"So we made it."

"We did."

They sat in silence.

Wilson said, "The question is: Made it to where? Another galaxy? A distant void?"

"Or another Universe."

"Yeah. That's the possibility I'd rather not think about."

"Where's the wormhole now?"

Wilson had not yet gained the presence of mind to think about that. "Not in front of us." Through the windshield vague images of galaxy clusters stretched across the cosmos. It all looked like delicate jewelry on black velvet.

"Deploying directional stabilizers," Clark said as he pressed the lever.

The ship turned around. Wilson switched on the video camera, and both men stared at the massive swirl of bluish white light streaks bending into a funnel. It looked just like what they'd seen going into the other side.

But now they were slowly moving away from it.

And they just watched.

Wilson didn't know what to think or what to say. Nothing could possibly be adequate.

His normally bold, adventurous-astronaut self felt as if it were desperately kicking away a dark monster, one he didn't want to admit: dread.

All the questions about wormholes and space-time flooded his mind. Now it was left to Clark and him to find out if they could go back through it the other way.

The dread that this may have been a one-way passage felt like the monster's grip clutching his chest. Exploring a vast emptiness was one thing. Being lost in it, on the other side of that wall, squeezed out his breath.

They slipped slowly and silently, farther and farther from the wormhole.

As if waking up to their reality, Wilson said, "Let's get the coordinates. If we can."

Something busy, something scientific, just something to do, was a relief. They scanned their location relative to the wormhole and typed in readings. Each piece of data started from scratch.

They established new coordinates and noted levels of gases, elements, and forces. Then they each leaned back. The question remained whether they could do anything about their data.

All systems of the ship were running normal. Wilson wouldn't have minded a major problem. It would have taken his mind away from his clamoring thoughts.

He wished for any kind of distraction, discovery, or intrusion—an inhabited planet, a space alien, anything but this vast emptiness on the other side of a wormhole.

And the nagging God-thought reemerged. After all this distance, God was nowhere to be seen. Why was he so maddeningly elusive?

Perhaps quantum physics held more answers than they'd realized: that if there were a God, he wouldn't inhabit the physical world or Universe at all. To create, he'd have to operate in a dimension beyond the creation. And it could very well intersect the one humans lived on, which would mean this God might be active right there on Earth—as Wilson had heard about the few times he'd been to church.

A thought pressed into Wilson's mind the way the force of the vortex had pressed into his chest: No matter how far he traveled, and whether he reached the edge of the Universe or went beyond it to a Multiverse, perhaps he had taken the wrong journey.

He looked into the little mirror glued to the console. There he was, in his sandy brown hair, gray-blue eyes looking back. The same him, just as he had been on Earth. And he wondered, instead of finding the edge of the Universe, maybe he'd found the edge of himself—where he was at fourteen and walking in the woods.

If that God could have intersected a person's existence on Earth, the same God could intersect Wilson's existence here, wherever *here* was.

He knew he did not have answers. And no more data would make a difference. In the face of this cosmos, the sophisticated ship was just a tin can.

In Wilson's pursuit of data and answers, he realized he had turned away from the wonder he once knew. And in so doing, he had turned away from God, away from the One God had sent.

Even if he never got back to Earth, he could still change course on what remained of his own life. This amazed him.

The memory that had cocooned him when he had gone unconscious may have been more than a coincidence. Regardless of whether he would die in endless space, the memory seemed to hold the portal—the wormhole—back to where his heart and mind needed to go.

He closed his eyes from the spectacle outside the window. And in his mind he went back, back, until he could see the forest, feel the fresh breeze. The breeze from heaven. He looked up. And the Universe coalesced back to the glistening pine needles and to the orchid.

For the first time in his life, it felt easy to pray.

Blood dripped from the lion's mouth
onto the gorged zebra.
"How terrible," said the woman
under her binoculars and safari hat.
But she had never lived with lions.

- 9 -

THE SURVIVOR

I glance down as the speedometer's passing 90. No helmet, of course. The sun's setting under a blushing sky, succumbing to darkness. Dark is good, closer to oblivion than light.

Leather-gloved hold on my Ninja 650, engine fever pitched. Hunched behind the windscreen, wind thundering over my head, I'm riding a rocket. A long, straight stretch, and I surge to 120, 130. Adrenaline pumping. A car in front of me. I pass it as if it's standing still—and the whoosh makes life feel almost worthwhile.

But I'll always have to stop. No matter how fast or how far, I'll eventually have to stop.

"Let me die," I whisper behind clenched teeth.

No, comes a voice.

I could try to pop a wheelie at 150—that might do it. Or go off a cliff—no cliffs here, just hills and valleys.

I said no.

I'm not drunk or high. And I'm not daydreaming. Speed clears the mind. Focuses it. And this kind of speed hacks off every peripheral thought. There can only be focus.

It's not your time.

"What the—" I'm not speaking to myself. Really I'm not.

I've been looking for a bridge abutment. That way no one else will get killed. I don't need to add more guilt onto my pile. A person shouldn't survive the way I did. I've ridden half an hour. Don't even know where I am. No bridges. Only farm fields and cow pastures. *Sheesh.* It's easier to kill yourself in the suburbs than in the countryside. I should've thought of that.

I will not take you. It's not yet your time.

I'm not speaking to myself. I may be suicidal, but I'm not a weirdo.

Neither am I. I'm astonishingly natural.

"Oh sure. Did God decide to talk to me?"

No.

"Then what?"

Nothing. Just the deafening wind over my screaming engine. Of course. What else would I expect?

I am Death.

"Whoa." I let go of the throttle and press the clutch and brake, 120—90—60—

I'm not at liberty to take you yet. But tempt me once more, and I'll let you be quadriplegic the rest of your life.

The voice pauses and I keep slowing, 40—20—10—

Physical debilitation is not in my department, but I could see that it's arranged.

I grind to a stop, stare at the pavement, then roll to the side of the road. Gravel crunches under the tires as the engine purrs. I'm panting, neck throbbing with a runaway pulse.

"Death doesn't talk to people. It just comes and . . ."

Generally that's true. You're one of the fortunate ones.

I look around just in case I might see some black phantom. Nothing.

Most people run from me and encase themselves with caution and insurance. People tempt me with the way they live, even the way they eat. They fight me, especially in intensive care units. Sometimes it wearies me. When I temporarily spare a life, they think they win; when I take a life, they think they lose. Strange creatures.

"Looks different from the other side, eh?"

Oh yes. The view is infinitely clearer. And here you are chasing me.

"Imagine that."

Yet your ambivalence contrasts your intent.

I don't ask what he means. Doesn't seem like a smart thing to do.

Now if you'll excuse me for a few years, I'll be on my way.

And the voice is gone, leaving me to wonder if I'm going crazy.

Whether that was real or my imagination, I can't keep going as if nothing happened. I turn off the engine, put the kickstand down, and get off. Beyond a barbed wire fence, a pasture stretches in front of me. Graying shades of green roll in the deepening dusk. A car whooshes behind me, the one I passed.

I sit and stare blankly at a cluster of cows on the far side of the pasture. Trees spread their umbrella canopies over thick black trunks.

And the never-ending replay shows itself again. Variations on the same theme. We sat in the café at the base PX until our whole squad had left. It was in Kallef, near the border. Just Scags, Ricky, and me. Ricky kept pinching the gal on duty until she threw a glass of water in his face. It was hilarious. I'd give a day's pay just to see that again. We sat there talking about our girlfriends back home and what we were going to do when our enlistments were up. Scags planned to go back to school, Ricky would join his father's business, and I, I was going to ride across the country and see whatever I saw. We sat there half the night until the Lieutenant finally came by and hauled us out. We were marines with a war to fight. Or maybe we were sacrificial lambs. Ricky never dreamed he'd have his legs blown off by an IED the next day. The rain fell so hard. That was the only day I remember it falling so hard—and why we got careless, thinking more about slipping in the mud than what was underneath it. Scags was in the rear, but I was standing just fourteen, fifteen yards from Ricky, and I caught a lot of shrapnel. It tore and burned through the skin as if I'd run through hell's gauntlet. I've got plenty of scars. But Ricky took it all. He screamed and gasped before he blacked out. Why did he get put on point? I should've been point; I had more experience.

The café gal never knew what happened. I wonder what she would have said if she did. I wonder if she would have let him pinch her one last time.

They kept Scags and me on the front until the end of August. We both came out with just scars. At least on the surface. A few weeks after we both came home, he stopped answering my calls. And my emails.

I still wake up at nights, seeing the flash and hearing the blast. Ricky's body flying above the fire. I can't get his scream out of my ears. I tell it to shut up, but it won't. I walk in the park and hear the scream behind me. I hear it from other drivers when I'm stopped at an intersection, and they blow up on the cross street in front of me. Then cars behind honk because I've got my eyes shut and my head against the steering wheel after the light turns green.

His body was shipped back and buried. After I got back, I visited his parents in San Diego to tell them everything I could about what a good marine and friend he'd been. I could hardly look at their faces, they kept tearing up, his mom clutching Ricky's portrait, her only son now just an image under a piece of glass. How does a mother imagine her child getting his legs blown off? What does she see in his face as he's bleeding out before a medic can come?

Scags and I tried to save him, but there was nothing to press down on to stop the blood, just a mass of shredded flesh. Sometimes when I wash my hands, I feel as if the blood still doesn't come off. The water streams down my fingers into the sink, the dirt comes off, but his blood seems soaked into the skin and never disappears.

Two cars pass, going the opposite direction I'm going. One's tailgating the other. Why am I concerned that it's dangerous?

The sky is darkening, the cows now a dim shadow. They become one dark blur against the trees. Never thought I'd envy cows.

Death is strange, but life is stranger.

I don't eat in restaurants any more. I just do takeout because I still see myself eating supper at that forward operating base. We were all tired and ready to sleep early. I got up to put my tray in the kitchen and get a cookie. Didn't hear a thing coming. Nobody outside saw or heard anything either. Then the explosion. The roof was only nylon fabric, and a mortar round hit the table where I was just sitting. The three guys still at the table were instantly killed. I just took more shrapnel and got thrown onto the dirt. If I had taken twenty seconds longer to eat, or if I had not wanted that cookie . . .

I should've died twice. I've been called a war hero, but it seems morally wrong for me to be alive.

So I act stupid.

I never took the trip across America. I got a job in maintenance for the local school district, and the adventure inside me sort of died. My parents were good to let me stay at home. But a man can't do that for long, so I got an apartment. A guy's supposed to suck things up and go on. The past is past. Create your own future.

Except when the past is like a pack of piranhas.

***

Three days later I go back to Fort Rosecrans Military
Cemetery, where I do penance for still being alive. It's
worth the hours of peace I get in return.

I park my bike along the main road and hang my helmet on the handlebars. Too many cops in the city to ride
with my head free. How intelligent I am—more afraid of
getting a ticket than of dying. I walk in. Greenest grass
anywhere, not a gopher mound in sight. Every gravestone
is 13 inches wide, just longer than my shoe, and rising
barely above my knee. Even in death we're at attention,
slabs of white marble set in ruler-straight lines, perfect
diagonals, and perfect rows straight on. Like dominoes.

I walk amid the stones toward the ocean, sun sparkling
off the water like an image of heaven itself. A navy ship is
passing toward the tip of Point Loma and into San Diego
Bay. The stones bear each guy's name, state he's from,
rank, branch of service, wars he fought in, dates of birth
and death. Most of them lived a full life. But not all.

Some of the more recent stones have phrases at the
bottom, like IN LOVING MEMORY, FOREVER IN OUR
HEARTS, IN GOD'S LOVING HANDS, FACE TO FACE WITH
JESUS. And then there are the ones for guys who aren't
quite sure they're dead: INTO THE WILD BLUE YONDER,
GONE FISHING, ALOHA, and TAKE IT EASY—Ummm . . .
a pilot, a fisherman, a Hawaiian, and a biker?

I find Ricky's stone.

At the bottom of his is SEMPER FI TOGETHER. And I begin to cry. I'm on my knees, bent over. Then I lift my face to the sky and curse because I don't know how I can be "always faithful together" with him. The marines never trained us for this.

So I sit staring across the white monuments to mortality, and at a woman dressed in black looking down at one.

I don't know why I say this out loud, but I do anyway: "Death! Where'd you go? I got a question!"

The woman looks at me. I hold up my hand and shake my head as if I were joking, as if I were not an idiot. Because only a moron would ask Death to come back to answer a question. The woman lets her gaze linger on me, then mercifully looks back down to the stone of the one taken from her.

Behind the woman spreads the sea. And now its glitter seems more like shattered bits of windshield glass strewn across asphalt.

The ship passes out of sight around the point. Two sailboats appear, moving the opposite way, north and out to sea. I wonder if they sail for the same kinds of reasons I ride, if it's their way of running from past dreams. Or chasing future ones.

I feel a stir in the air. I tense.

It's you again.

"Death? You really came?" I'm not sure I believe it.

I've been busy on the freeway.

"What happened there?"

It doesn't matter what happened. *The end result is always the same. Only the living are concerned about what happened.*

"Some of us never stop thinking about it."

And you live in bondage. But death is not *a good way out.*

"Rather irreversible, I suppose."

You intrigue me. You're not afraid of me the way most are.

"I have nothing to lose. Nothing to gain."

Ah, but you have much to lose and much to gain. The ignorance of the living, like yours, never ceases to amuse me.

"I'm so glad I'm good for something."

Your eternity—be it good or bad—is infinitely greater than you imagine. At best you're looking at it through a peephole of despair. You're a foreigner to the afterlife. You've no idea of the reality.

"Okay. But what about Ricky's reality? What did you do with him after you took him?"

It's not your business.

"I don't care. Where did he go?"

I like your audacity.

"Did he go to a better place like I hear about?"

A better place?

It sounds as if Death snorts after he says that.

Nonsense.

"What then?"

As with everyone else, I turned him over to the Almighty.

"What does he do with Ricky, with everyone?"

He gave you The Book to read. You'd solve a lot of your problems if you read The Book.

"The Book . . . ? What, you mean the Bible? That's just fairy tales."

I might be imagining it, but I'm certain two fiery eyes glare at me, ready to scorch me.

"Okay. I'll . . . read it."

Good. People live their whole lives as if I didn't exist. Or as if the Almighty were comatose. Then they get upset when I come to take them. They live foolishly then vainly hope for more chances after it's too late. If more had your kind of bravado, my job would be far more interesting.

"I'll take that as a compliment."

As only someone like you would. Yet your heart is still broken. You were cursing about not being able to fulfill the wish on Ricky's stone.

"Yes. How can I be Semper Fi together with him?"

Imagine Death giving advice on how to live.

"It does seem ludicrous. But I can't think of anyone more qualified."

Hmmm. You're not such a fool. I'll let you in on this much: I will come for you later than you hope and sooner than you expect. So quit messing around.

"Oka-a-a-y . . ."

Until that time will you waste every day wishing you didn't have it? Or will you live on Ricky's behalf the life he could not? Live for both of you.

My thoughts halt as if for a stop sign, and my body is gently shaking. The lady in black walks past me up to the road.

And—I think—I start to see. I have no answers. But I may be starting to see.

I wrap my arms around the stone, pull myself tight to it. "Semper Fi together, Ricky. I'll figure it out."

Now you're getting it. When we meet again, I think you'll be ready.

And I nod.

The Latin term *Semper Fidelis* means "always faithful" and is the motto of the United States Marine Corps, often abbreviated to *Semper Fi.*

This story is dedicated to all those who have died in, and to those who have survived, America's wars.

"Bang! Bang! You're dead!" shouted Johnny.

"No, I'm not!" snapped Chucky.

And the world waited for Chucky to be right.

- 10 -

THE FORGIVER

Shireen's heart pounded as hard as her feet.

None of this was happening. It couldn't be for real. It was all too—that word she'd just learned—*insane*.

She stopped for a bicycle rickshaw passing in front of her and kept running toward the park. No. Papa said bad men might do bad things to her there. Ah, Mr. Varghese's shop just beyond the park. He was kind to her, and in the back he had a small courtyard where he drank tea with favorite customers, like Papa. She turned left around the corner then darted across a side street and into the alley, where she found Mr. Varghese's red gate. Shireen remembered it well from the times she'd come with Papa. The gate was unlocked, and she crept in. She perched on the same wrought iron chair where she sometimes sat with Papa while he drank tea with Mr. Varghese. "The best tea of India," the man always said, his eyes seeming to smile above his bushy mustache.

She wished he were sitting with her now.

Or maybe not. She needed to be alone, completely alone.

Her heartbeat gradually slowed, but her mind felt ready to explode. She shook her head until her brain throbbed and neck hurt.

Pinching her eyes shut, plugging her ears, talking out loud—nothing could push the searing images and sounds from her memory. . . .

***

"You're ugly!" Abdul had said.

But other boys said the same kinds of things to girls. And almost all the boys said and did worse things to each other.

But then Abdul said, "You smell. Like all Hindus."

Of course she told her mother. She told her mother everything that happened at school. If Abdul had said she smelled sweet, she would have told her mother. But when she said, "like all Hindus," her mother froze and stared at the wall. The dishes in her hands rattled ever so slightly. At first Shireen felt comforted because she could tell her mother felt bad about it too, so Shireen wouldn't have to feel bad by herself. But when her mother turned, she could see the whites in her bulging eyes. And the eyebrows arced up, the way they did when Mother was angry, and creased the red *bindi* spot on her forehead.

Then Mother yelled, *"He said you smelled? Like all Hindus?"*

Poonish and Bansi raced into the kitchen as fast as if someone had shouted, *Fire!* Poonish demanded the details: "When did he say it?"

"At lunch recess."

"Did he say anything else?"

"That I was ugly."

"What happened before that?"

"He threw a rubber ball at me and hit my shoulder."

"An aggressor! Attacking my little sister!"

Her cousin Bansi was like a brother to Poonish. Bansi listened, nodding in agreement. He did not say a word, but his eyes narrowed.

Abdul was a Muslim.

The room fell quiet. Poonish's chest rose and fell with heavy breaths, as if the rage in her mother's eyes had jumped to him. His lips pressed tightly the way they did whenever he was mad and about to react.

Mother stared coldly at the floor and put her arm around Shireen.

When Shireen realized what was happening, her breath halted. "No, Poonish! It's okay. Abdul didn't mean it. He was just playing." But Abdul did mean it. Whether he was playing or not didn't matter.

The muscles on the side of Bansi's face contracted and twitched. His eyes were still narrow.

"No Muslim insults my sister or my people and gets away with it," Poonish said.

"No one," echoed Bansi.

They turned to leave, and Shireen reached to stop them, but her mother held her back.

Shireen peered at her, but she only said, "They will take care of it. Do your homework."

"Yes, Mother."

No, Mother.

She should not have obeyed her mother. But she always did. She was a good girl, and Mother would have slapped her if she hadn't obeyed. Papa had taken a train to New Delhi, where he was staying in a hotel and meeting with important people, people who worked for the government. He might have known what to do, might have let her disobey.

This one time, for the first time, she should have disobeyed. She should have run after Poonish and Bansi. She should have grabbed the gun.

Papa's gun was supposed to be used only for protection if a robber came. But Poonish and Bansi took it and marched to Abdul's house. They did not know how to be calm the way Papa did.

She imagined Abdul's round face and how it had sneered at her. But how many other boys—Hindu boys—had done the same? She also saw Abdul's scowl turn to a smile, a broad, toothy grin, full of life.

Until Poonish returned. "Two bullets, in his head." He said it so confidently, his chin held high. Then he set the gun back in the closet as if that were the end of the problem.

Shireen couldn't breathe.

She closed her eyes and brought back Abdul's face, so full of life—but now blotted out by two holes and a widening circle of blood. Bullets were such small things, yet they caused so much horror. And they didn't make problems end. They seemed to make them worse. Everything always seemed to get worse.

Moments later the knock on the door was so loud, Shireen jumped. A man's voice shouted to open the door. Poonish and Bansi yelled back. Several voices outside shouted again. Shireen ran to her room, shut the door, and cowered behind the wardrobe, squeezing her knees to her chest. The knocking changed to pounding. She felt the vibrations all the way back in her room. A crack of wood.

More beating. Another crack, and the sound of the front door slamming open against the wall. A gun shot, maybe Papa's. Yelling. Pots breaking, furniture crashing, more shouting. Shireen's door had no lock. She prayed to no god in particular that nobody would come through the door. The shouting and beating and breaking went on and on. She covered her ears, closed her eyes, and buried her face in her light blue dress. Her whole body shuddered, and tears soaked through the dress fabric and into her knees.

Then came her mother's scream—piercing the air, piercing Shireen's soul.

She waited for Mother to stop. But Mother kept screaming between gulping breaths and did not stop. Shireen forced herself up and toward the door. She gingerly turned the knob and peeked out. No yelling or beating or smashing. The people seemed to have gone. She tiptoed into the hallway. Broken chairs and pots covered the floor. In the midst of it all, lay a pair of legs. She crept farther and gasped. Another pair. Mother wailed and convulsed forward and back over the bodies of Poonish and Bansi. Their heads were beaten so badly that the skulls had caved in and didn't look like heads anymore. Pools of blood spread and converged into one.

Shireen stumbled toward her mother but could go no farther than the corpses. She could not breathe, could not move.

Voices came from outside. One by one, men gathered at the open door. Her next-door neighbor, his wife and son behind him, a man down the street, others she did not know.

Mother kept shrieking and rocking.

Shireen felt a wet tickle around her bare feet and looked down to see them surrounded by the blood. Poonish's blood, Bansi's blood.

Her insides seemed to break and her stiffness exploded. She screamed. Bolted past her mother, past the neighbors, and down the street.

Her heart pounded as hard as her feet.

None of this was happening. It couldn't be for real. Poonish and Bansi couldn't be dead. It was all too insane.

She stopped for a bicycle rickshaw passing in front of her, ran past the park and into an alley toward the courtyard behind Mr. Varghese's store. She opened the red gate and sat on one of the wrought iron chairs.

The thoughts and images of one single afternoon and evening crashed on her like a falling building. She would go back and find it was all a bad dream, a bad vision like the Brahmin priests warned about. But she bent down and rubbed her finger between her toes. The moon offered enough dim light to see that what came off on her finger was indeed the blood of her brother and cousin.

Shireen sat until the moon had drifted past a tree next door. The outlines of leaves spread pitch black against the dark sky. Blackness against darkness, as if it knew how she felt. Yet the thought made her shudder, and she shrank with her hands over her head. She wanted no one to find her. Not even Mother.

She wanted to redo the past day. Start over. Tell Abdul to say something different or he would get two bullets and her brother and cousin would get clubs.

She wished and wished. But days never started over.

Well, then she would disappear. She rummaged through what Mr. Varghese had piled in a corner and pulled out a blue tarp. She wrapped it around herself like a cocoon and lay down. Maybe by the time the sun rose, she would be gone, or have turned into another person. Or maybe something else, like a butterfly.

***

Shireen felt the warmth of the sun through the bright blue all around her. Voices and bicycle bells rang in the alley, and the grind of truck engines drifted from the main street on the other side of the store. Of course she could not disappear.

But she couldn't be who she was anymore. Not after yesterday. Not ever.

Shireen unrolled herself, hoping Mr. Varghese hadn't come yet or would be too busy in the store to come out for tea. She folded and replaced the tarp. He would never know.

She stood at the gate, wanting to open it but not knowing what to do if she did.

She would not go to school.

She would not go home.

If only she could go to Abdul's house. Tell his family she was sorry. That she wished Abdul was still alive. Cry with them. Hold Abdul's body and pray that the bullets would come out and his life return.

But his life would not return, the bullets would stay, and it did not matter that she was sorry.

His people did not forgive those kinds of things. Nor did hers. At least in her town. A few years earlier Hindus and Muslims had rioted and killed each other over an argument about land that both sides said was holy to them. The government sent in the army, and the land sat fenced off ever since.

Tears streamed down her cheeks. "I want to die," she whimpered. She held her hand to her trembling chest. If only she could die, she wouldn't have to live through the day, or any after that. She looked at the gate latch but could not make herself open it. There was nowhere to go.

A bird landed on a branch in the tree next door. It cocked its head and chirped, as if to interrupt her.

She wondered what it might tell her if it could speak, since chirping birds always seemed to carry a message of hope.

But hope was to her like someone else's useless song on the radio.

The bird persisted in its song.

Then the thought came to her: If she couldn't change what had happened, could she change what *would* happen?

What if she forgave even when no one else did? She had never been taught how to forgive because that would show weakness. But maybe the grownups were not right. Just as Mother was not right to let Poonish and Bansi go off with the gun.

Then Shireen remembered.

The man who stretched his arms out on a plus sign. The man the Christians worshiped.

Mama told her that those people were no better than untouchables. Yet the man with outstretched arms forgave. Yes, that was what he did. He forgave people.

She smiled at the bird. It cocked its head again and flitted away.

She felt as if she had just woken up and could breathe again.

Shattering glass. She jumped. Then screeching tires. Honking horns. Shouting. More breaking glass.

No. She reached for the gate latch. *Let this be about something else. It's already too bad.*

She lifted the latch and stepped into the alley, where several boys were running. She followed them. Boys always went toward things that were happening, not away from them. Around a corner and onto the main street.

She stopped and gasped.

Men were fist fighting one another in the middle of the halted traffic. Others came with sticks.

No. She shook her head. *Please let this not be because of what happened yesterday.* But by the insults they hurled at each other, she knew the answer was yes.

A potbellied man came out of a shop with a broken window. He lifted a gun and shot in the air. No one ran away. Instead, one man ran to him and grabbed the gun out of his hands then shot the potbellied man in the chest.

Shireen's breath caught in her throat, suppressing a silent scream.

Two men jumped on the man with the gun and wrestled him to the ground. Then more came, kicking and stomping until the man lay still.

She was jolted loose when another window smashed and sprayed glass shards. She slowly turned in a circle. All around her men yelled at each other, carrying sticks and rocks and bottles.

On the other side of the street two men faced off. Each held a machete and waved it at the other while shouting. One wore a white Muslim *kufi* cap; the other the sash of a Hindu.

They were preparing to kill each other.

And no one was stopping them.

Shireen walked toward them. Feet pricked from pebbles and broken glass. Poonish and Bansi's blood still smeared between her toes. Wearing the same light blue dress she had on when she was with Abdul in the schoolyard.

She stopped, took a deep breath, and spread her arms straight out right and left like the man on the plus sign.

"I forgive you," she said.

No one heard.

Louder, "I forgive you!"

A man grabbed her arm from behind. "Get away, little girl. You'll get hurt."

She yanked it back and glared at him.

He blinked several times and gaped at her as if she were an alien.

No one knew who she was. This all started with her, and no one even knew her. *Insane,* she thought.

Of course this had all started long before her. Papa and her uncles sometimes talked about the fighting. She had merely opened the wound.

She had to close it.

"Shireen!"

Mr. Varghese stood under a tree, holding his arms toward her. Today his bushy mustache was twitching, and his sparkling eyes seemed to cry. Dear Mr. Varghese.

She forced a trembling smile, bowed her head, and turned back to the machete wavers. They stepped back and forth, threatening and cursing. She spread out her arms once more and marched straight at them.

"Shireen!" came Mr. Varghese's cry again.

But she was no longer the girl who sat at Papa's side in the courtyard.

Right between the two men. Under their machetes.

With all her breath, as loudly as she could, she bellowed, *"I forgive you!"*

She waited for steel blades to sever her arms. When she felt none, she looked one man in the eye. "I forgive you." Then the other, "I forgive you."

Each backed away, lowered his machete, and gawked at her as if she were crazy.

She stood firm until they turned their backs a safe distance away.

Without thinking, she marched toward a melee of fists and feet, stretched her arms, and pushed her now-emptied self into the crush. A blow to the side of her head sent shockwaves through her and knocked her to her knees. She forced herself up. A foot stomped her bare toes, and they hurt so much, she thought they'd break off. An elbow hit her stomach, another her back. The wind knocked out of her, she could not speak. But she pressed into the center and held her arms straight out.

The pain throbbed so badly she kept her eyes shut. Yet she felt the men pull apart. She reeled as she opened her eyes to see the men all stepping away and staring at her. With only a whisper of breath left, and arms still spread, she mouthed the words.

She staggered from one fist and stick and rock to another, rasping the words, stretching her arms.

Voice by voice, the shouting quieted. Weapons lowered and eyes watched as she zigzagged among the rioters.

The entire street grew quiet.

She stopped in the middle, looked back at the people staring, and . . . and . . . she had no idea what to do.

Her breath returned enough to shout, "I forgive you!" Again, "I forgive you!" Perhaps they could learn from a girl. Or from the man who forgave people.

And maybe—she hoped—their hearts might break too.

Shireen closed her eyes and prayed. In her mind's eye she could see Abdul smile.

This story is a fictional take on real situations and events in northern India.

May there be more people like Shireen.

ABOUT THE AUTHOR

Peter Lundell is a pastor, Bible college teacher, and writer who helps people connect with God and live well in the face of eternal reality. With missionary and teaching experience all over the world, he brings new perspectives to what most people overlook. He holds an M.Div. and D.Miss. from Fuller Theological Seminary and has authored books and articles on prayer, revival, and spiritual warfare. He writes nonfiction, fiction, and collaborative books. Visit him at www.PeterLundell.com for his weekly blog, online library, and inspirational "Connections."

Appendix

Thoughts and Questions for Personal Reflection or Group Discussion

1. FAR ENCOUNTER

I wrote this story out of experiences in Haiti, where I rode a motorcycle through the rough roads of rural Haiti. And I visited a lot of Haitians in their mud huts. I imagined what might have happened if I had popped a wheelie and landed wrong.

Too often people superficially assume that those of high socio-economic status, like the American Sean, maintain cultural superiority over those of low socio-economic status, like the Haitian Angelique. Occasionally things happen that force us to see beyond our misconceptions. What blinds us to the good points of other people and cultures? What opens our eyes and hearts?

How do you respond to this story?

What personal experience does this story remind you of?

In what way does the story speak to you?

2. THE DANCER

I have a friend who has arthritis in her feet. I wondered, What if such a person were a senior citizen who had once been a ballet dancer? How could one experience gracefulness or vitality despite the ravages of aging? While thinking of that, I received an advertisement in the mail for *The Nutcracker* ballet, and I began to write. Then I went with my wife to see the performance.

Psalm 139 says we are "fearfully and wonderfully made." Though our bodies and abilities diminish with age, some things surely endure inside us. And within limitations our passions can still find expression, or at least I hope so. Can people with a will, like Grace, still feel and deeply enjoy the sense and the exhilaration of what they once did physically? Even within the ravages of debilitating illness, like Ralph's stroke, is there a place between the heart and mind where long-lost exuberance can still come to life?

How do you respond to this story?

What personal experience does this story remind you of?

In what way does the story speak to you?

3. IN THE RING

This story is a surrealist allegory, originally intended to be the opening chapter of an otherwise nonfiction book on God's seeming absence when we're hurting and how to connect with him in the midst of the pain. There were already so many books on the subject that the manuscript never got published (at least not yet). So, here's the story.

Sometimes we think we're fighting or wrestling with God, when we're really fighting with ourselves. We are often our own worst enemy. We may think God is against us, when we really suffer from our own thinking and behavior. Amazingly, God lets us go on like this as long as we choose to. Life is complicated, but cutting through to core issues, we may often find ourselves in the place of the boxer. Have you?

How do you respond to this story?

What personal experience does this story remind you of?

In what way does the story speak to you?

4. TURNING POINT

I long had an image in the back of my mind of a person sitting at the hospital bedside of another person dying. I wondered what would happen, and how the visitor might be changed by the experience.

Countless people, like Sophie, can get caught up in narcissistic materialism and naïvely ignore those who suffer. They may also be oblivious to the notion of giving to others. This story takes that disconnect to a stark dramatization and conclusion in the case of Leonard. What would make someone like Leonard do what he did?

How do you respond to this story?

What personal experience does this story remind you of?

In what way does the story speak to you?

5. ANNA'S TREASURES

I twice taught in Vladivostok, Russia's far-eastern harbor city. I saw old, pre-revolution houses and buildings overlooking the modern harbor and imagined what it would have been like to be bourgeois and either have to escape or face death with the Bolsheviks after Red October in 1917 and the rise of Communism. Then I wondered what life would have been like in the new country.

Materialism can blind and diminish the soul of a person. We typically notice people who amass material goods. Yet what about those, like Anna, who obsess over what they want but fall short of their desires? Contrasting that are those, like Sergei, who see the emptiness of such a life and instead turn to faith and relationships.

How do you respond to this story?

What personal experience does this story remind you of?

In what way does the story speak to you?

6. BRONZE MAN

Walter Wangerin's short story "Rag Man" got my imagination going on giving away body parts for the benefit of others. I turned it around to have the Christ figure employ the body parts of others. Depicting a real-world story at the beginning and the end created a stronger effect than when I initially had it only as a dream.

God calls people to sacrificially give themselves to his greater purposes in the world, in this example, faith-based urban renewal. To put things in a biblical dimension, consider the parallel between the bronzed apocalyptic Son of God (who sacrificed himself for us), the bronze altar (where the sacrifice was made) and the call of believers to offer themselves as living sacrifices. Those who do so identify with "the Bronze Man" as they serve—and receive back the enhancement of whatever they give.

How do you respond to this story?

What personal experience does this story remind you of?

In what way does the story speak to you?

7. THE WONDER OF OG

I wanted to develop the idea of an intellectual caveman who saw past the things contemporaries merely accepted. Why do we always assume people who lived in caves were stupid? I imagined a thoughtful caveman who in his primitive way had a deep and tender love for his wife and child and asked endless profound questions.

What is ultimate truth and meaning, and where do we find it? What happens when we push beyond pervasive religious assumptions and practices and insist that a greater spiritual reality lies beyond what's commonly practiced? In a setting stripped of modern institutions, contrivances, and ideologies—down to the barest notion of being human—Og is a model of one who has a passion for truth and meaning. He intuitively knows he can ultimately find it only in "the Great God," and he'll do anything to connect with that.

How do you respond to this story?

What personal experience does this story remind you of?

In what way does the story speak to you?

8. JOURNEY TO THE EDGE

The Universe is said to have an edge that expands—or some say contracts—and is thought to somehow curve back into itself. There are also theories of other universes, or a Multiverse. In the midst of that are the theorized wormholes that may link different dimensions of space and are possibly traversable. I wanted to contrast a scientific, data-oriented approach with a more spiritually minded view that reaches beyond data to the original source.

Do we really imagine God is out there somewhere—as if he were a physical being hanging out in the cosmos? If God is a spiritual being, wouldn't we encounter him in a spiritual way? And wouldn't that way be as available in the simplicities of nature as in outer space? We should be wise in the kinds of life journeys we take and what we expect from them.

How do you respond to this story?

What personal experience does this story remind you of?

In what way does the story speak to you?

9. THE SURVIVOR

I had the war images in my mind for a long time and later wondered at the epidemic of veterans with PTSD and their high suicide rates. I tried to get inside the mind of one and what it might be like, and the motorcycle offered a good way to do it. I had two marine veterans check the story for accuracy of details and of the combat experience. One of them rides a motorcycle like the one in the story. Then I wondered what it would be like if the spirit of death were to be friendly and talk to us.

What self-destructive things do people do when they live with emotional pain? We normally don't think of talking with or learning from the spirit of death, but in the story Death teaches the narrator about living well in the face of eternal reality. Can you think of more ways we can learn things like this?

How do you respond to this story?

What personal experience does this story remind you of?

In what way does the story speak to you?

10. THE FORGIVER

I spent two months in India and got to know the people and the country a little bit. Many years later I read news of a town in northern India where a Muslim boy and Hindu girl had a schoolyard spat. Her family members shot the boy. The boy's family retaliated. Then Muslims and Hindus rioted and killed one another. I wondered what might have happened if someone had intervened with the forgiveness of the guy on the "plus sign."

Forgiveness sometimes demands strength to the point of self-sacrifice, especially when it comes between two groups separated by entrenched animosity. Though Shireen doesn't know the name of the despised Christians' God, he becomes her source of hope. The implicit question is whether these two groups, or others like them, are willing to follow Jesus' example and forgive as well. I don't encourage you to hold your breath on this.

How do you respond to this story?

What personal experience does this story remind you of?

In what way does the story speak to you?